DANCING
❊ DAYS ❊

To J.C.D. –
the Head Man

I will pour out my spirit on all flesh.

Your sons and your daughters shall prophesy,

Your old men shall dream dreams,

And your young men shall see visions.

The Whitsun Canticle,
taken from the Acts of the Apostles, chapter 2 verse 17

❈ CONTENTS ❈

❊ DANCING DAYS ❊
Characters in order of appearance

DR WOOLF (THE WOLF)	Headmaster of Worthington College. (1)
JOHNNY CLARKE	Protagonist; a member of the Lower Sixth at Worthington.
NICK	A member of the Lower Sixth at Worthington.
BILLY	A member of the Lower Sixth at Worthington. (1)
ANGUS	A member of the Lower Sixth at Worthington, and Johnny's best friend.
LUIGI	Nick's 'fag'.
MR MORSE (THE HORSE)	Johnny's housemaster.
MR BURKINSHAW (THE BURK)	Classics master; Johnny's tutor.
MR HAWKE (THE HAWK)	Master in charge of the Waggery.
MRS HAWKE	His wife.
ANGELA	Angus' girlfriend.
JANE BAXTER	Johnny's beloved.
TINA THE TUCKER	Serving girl in school tuck shop.
SERGEANT FROST (ERF)	Field Day platoon commander.
MR and MRS BAXTER	Proprietors of the Rose and Crown at Bockington and parents of Jane.
DR CUST	Stand-in Latin master.
GREG GLASS	A member of the Lower Sixth.
TOM BENNETT	Pupil at Clouds; fellow-pupil of Johnny's at prep school. (1)
MR KENDAL	Headmaster of Clouds.
EVA and ARABELLA	Pupils at Clouds.
THE REV and MRS CLARKE	Johnny's parents. (1)
STEVE	Leader of the visiting Borstal boys.

(1) denotes appearance in Volume 1 of
   THE SONS OF THE MORNING sequence: *A STORM OF CHERRIES.*

DANCING
❃ DAYS ❃

❈ CHAPTER 1 ❈

An
Announcement

O n the first morning of the summer term the school assembled in Great Hall. The Headmaster addressed the boys and this is what he said:

'Deriving much of their tradition and many of their practices from the monastic orders, public schools have always been of single sex.'

This last word instantly stirred a measure of interest in his hearers.

'The process of opening our somewhat enclosed society has already begun, with the introduction of free-place boys.'

This referred to the recent admission into the school of a small number of youths from the locality. Their accents and enthusiasm had made integration difficult.

'There is greater freedom of access to the outside world.'

The senior boys thought fondly of the pubs in Bishopstown.

'Weekend exeats have been increased in number.'

It was not clear who favoured this. Certainly some parents had muttered that they did not pay to send their children to boarding school in order to have to fetch them home every other weekend.

'There is the school dance with St Agnes.'

A light snigger passed through the company.

'And there is the Borstal exchange.'

Under this, boys from the local juvenile remand centre spent a few days at the College, where they marvelled ceaselessly at the poverty and antiquity of the facilities, the rigorousness of its authoritarian structure and relentless academic routine.

'But all these, though significant in themselves,' the Head, Dr Woolf, continued, 'are mere garnishing to what remains essentially the same dish. Whereas what the governors and I have now decided upon and what, when it becomes truly established, will make a profound change in the very nature of Worthington, is nothing less than the introduction of girls into our Sixth Form, as full residential members of the school. In September year, as I stand here, I shall be addressing you not as 'boys' only but 'boys and girls.' Although one or two public schools have already embarked on this novel course it will be a daring innovation in a school so strongly founded on the Anglican church tradition.'

Here the boys reflected, glumly in most cases, on the compulsory chapel attendance that formed so regular and frequent a feature of their lives. 'It will be a turning point in the school's history. It is not yet certain how many girls there will be, whether they will occupy quarters already available in the school or have their own purpose-built accommodation, or which member of staff will be in charge of them. These are matters to which we will be busily putting our minds in the coming months. But the essential point is decided: Worthington's Sixth Form is to become co-educational.'

This pronouncement was greeted by the school with profound silence as at the news of a sudden and shocking death. The other elements of the Headmaster's speech such as mundane details of the forthcoming summer term were received indifferently, like the minor details of a will that follow the part concerning oneself.

Johnny Clarke and his friends drifted away from Great Hall, stunned. Wordlessly grouped together they drifted naturally to Nick's study, their usual place of resort. This was more a suite of rooms than the customary public school cell denoted by that word. It was situated in the basement of his house and along with the other former studies there, which had in an even earlier era accommodated bachelor staff, had officially been rendered redundant by the recent building of a light and airy study block, fit only, in Nick's words, 'for battery hens'. Nick preferred the spacious darkness of the basement and had somehow contrived to make territorial claims there which neither his Head of House nor his Housemaster, Mr Morse, were courageous enough to contest, so forceful and unusual was Nick's character. He thus, in what had been the living quarters of half a dozen boys, enjoyed accommodation sufficient for a small family. This included cooking facilities – a double gas ring (the school's), augmented by a small gas stove (his own) and of course a bathroom and lavatory. Of natural light there was little and of ventilation – unless the outside door be open – none. In the winter months it had been marvellously snug by virtue of the huge heating pipes that passed through it at ceiling height from the boiler room next door. The warmth and sunshine of summer, however – though the introduction of a refrigerator promised cooling refreshment – threatened to render it stuffy and claustrophobic.

'Well, I think it's incredible,' Johnny remarked, when they were comfortably seated with their coffee. This non-committal exclamation was intended as a conversation starter rather than as comment of any value in itself, Johnny not aspiring to be an opinion-former in the group. Nick swayed comfortably in his rocking chair and Angus inspected his host's new collection of *avant-garde* posters adorning the walls. Billy, black in pigment and saturnine by nature, lay along the back of the chesterfield, scowling. 'Bloody incredible,' Johnny repeated, his first exclamation having received no response.

'I think it's a bloody good idea,' said Angus, moving restlessly about the room. He was really hoping for an appearance by Luigi, Nick's unofficial fag, on whom he had a crush. The instinctive host, indulgently providing for the appetites of his guests, Nick called out, 'Luigi! – the chocolate biscuits.'

'Bloody incredible!'

'Shut up, Johnny.'

Enter Luigi, a small boy of astonishing mediterranean beauty, with the biscuits. His father, the proprietor of an expensive London restaurant, was well known to Nick and had appealed to him to look after his son at school, which he had chosen entirely because Nick attended it. This responsibility Nick took conscientiously and protected the boy from any unwelcome attentions, partly by keeping him in almost constant attendance upon himself. The responsibility was further lightened not by the olive skin and dark brown eyes by which Angus was smitten and to which he was indifferent but by Luigi's provision, through his father, of colossal supplies of food and drink and by his own precocious skill in cooking. On the gas rings and the little electric stove Luigi worked culinary wonders and Nick had not eaten in the dining hall for two terms.

'Christ!' Johnny laughed. 'I just can't imagine it. I mean – sitting next to you – in class!'

Johnny had provoked little conversational response. Angus, who might have joined in these thoughts, was preoccupied with offering to do Luigi's Latin prep for him during the new term. And Nick and Billy rarely stooped to barefaced wonderment such as Johnny was now so ingenuously expressing.

'Don't get too excited, Johnny,' said Nick. 'After all, you won't be here when they do arrive.'

'Yes, I will – Oxbridge term.'

'Yes,' Angus now joined in on Luigi's exit, 'and I might stay on for another term after that, if there's this incentive.'

'It's not natural,' was Nick's view, 'packing boys together till the age of sixteen and then suddenly unleashing the full flood of femininity upon them. A terrible shock to the psycho-sexual system. Better have them from the start or not at all.'

At Worthington there was an almost total absence of female company and influence. There were some Housemasters' wives who could be seen wearing plastic macintoshes as they carried flowers into chapel or hustled small children out of old estate cars, their cardiganned bosoms offering much of mothering and nothing of sex. Matron and her assistant, through long trafficking with boys' pyjamas, had transcended femininity as such: 'You can't shock me,' was Matron's robust response to some character's ill-considered exhibition of his sexuality. There had been two daughters of a master whose occasional appearance in chapel on Sunday morning had lent that occasion a less than religious effulgence in the eyes of many of the boys, one of whom had actually contrived to go out with the prettier girl. Having since left the school, he was rumoured to have married her which rather took the romance out of it. But that was all, apart from Tina at the school tuck shop ('Tina the Tucker') whose hairy chin above a swelling bosom gave conflicting evidence as to the gender to which she naturally belonged. Thus the female sex in the average Worthingtonian mind was something of a coarse joke, it being divided into three groups: mothers, hags and sex-objects.

'What do you think, Billy?'

Johnny turned to the one of their number who had real status in the sexual field. Though not above the local variety of passion – a tall blond boy in the Remove had been less than discreet about their relationship – Billy hailed from an African country where sexual intercourse was commonplace amongst his people from the age of about ten, or so he said. He had even hinted that he himself was already betrothed but this was not believed. More fascinating were remarks about the nature of sex education in his family as this appeared to involve the procurement by his mother of sexual partners for him and his initiation by them. Johnny could not but contrast this with his own experience of sex education at home. The Rectory contained several colourful paperbacks, the products of religious publishing houses, on whose covers youthful couples skipped hand-in-hand through meadows, laughing their lust away. 'Romance, yes: sex, no' appeared to be the message. Disapproval and fascination vied in Johnny's mind at the image of Billy's member which, neither concealed nor flaunted, was of such dimensions as to corroborate his claims.

Billy's reply was terse. 'Fuck 'em,' he said.

The remorseless return to routine of the first day of term was alleviated later that evening by a little brandy, provided by Nick (or rather, Luigi). Nick was still eating his apricot sorbet when the others came in from a school supper of scotch egg and boiled potatoes followed by bread and jam. But the coffee was already percolating and some glimpses of civilisation began to reassert themselves after a day of hanging up cricket flannels and writing one's name in new Latin texts. Nick was not expected to provide for everyone, but he knew when to be generous. The company sniffed and sipped at their cognac like suffocating men at an oxygen tank. Johnny was seated on his favourite item of Nick's furniture – a modern thing, a sort of baggy cushion, shapeless in itself, whose loose granular contents were compacted on receipt of an occupant into firm contours of support. It rustled slightly under him and changed shape as he moved.

The topic of the introduction of girls was resumed.

'Consider the political view,' Billy offered.

'What do you mean?' asked Johnny.

'Perhaps I meant the socio-organisational point of view.'

'He means Who's going to be in charge?' explained Nick. 'There are no female members of staff so unless it is proposed to appoint one for the purpose – which is not impossible – there will have to be a master in charge.'

'A female member of staff? Christ!'

'And if it is a master in charge – who?'

Various names were instantly canvassed but Nick persisted in his more systematic approach. 'It must be somebody not already in an important administrative position – obviously not a Housemaster or even Senior Subject Master. So, an Assistant Housemaster perhaps.'

'What about the Dove?' suggested Johnny. All members of

staff were popularly designated by a proper or common noun preceded by the definite article. The name was not necessarily descriptive but there was always some perceivable aptness to it, as in the Wolf (Dr Woolf); the Dove (Mr Doverne); the Horse (their housemaster whose name, Morse, combined with a certain long-faced quality and a neighing laugh to provide this sobriquet); the Cow, his wife – and so on.

'The Dove?' Nick considered his candidature. 'Too wet. You must remember that this is 'a turning point'.' Nick was here quoting but did not descend to imitating the Wolf. 'It is vital that the innovation should be a success.'

'The Hawk?'

'Too new. He's got to have someone with a bit of form. What do you think, Billy?'

Billy was inscrutable a moment as all eyes turned on him. Then, 'The Burk,' he said.

The possibility of the appointment of the man thus denoted was so appalling that only silence could follow his nomination.

Mr Burkinshaw, assumed by his accent to be of northern extraction, had joined the school quite some years before. Slow to gain recognition in a more gentlemanly and colourful Common Room, he had nonetheless over the years established himself by his willingness to perform tasks generally avoided by his colleagues. He was of unpleasing appearance. Though not old (even by the boys' standards) he stooped and was virtually bald. His scalp, prematurely defoliated as if by a vicious chemical misapplied, glistened whitely like the breeding ground of some microscopic fungal growth: it certainly didn't do to look too closely. His flagrant Christianity – he was a daily attender at early communion in the crypt – was also against him. Johnny was less antipathetic to him than most, having been prepared for Greek O Level by him with an enthusiasm salted with pedantry that he found both repellent and sustaining. His pass in the subject had been largely due, he privately considered, to the Burk, so that, though he was condoled over it, he was not altogether dismayed at finding himself allotted to him under the tutorial system the Wolf had recently established. Johnny didn't like the man but had to admit that in his ghastly way he meant well.

'He'll work like hell to set it all up,' Nick continued. 'He'll fight like mad for his charges as a good housemaster should. He'll bully good work out of them, keep them out of mischief and paint the bloody bathrooms if he has to. He'll die in the cause if need be. Billy's right – the Burk's the man.'

Behind the Horse's raspberry canes shortly afterwards Johnny and Angus smoked the first cigarette of the term.

'I don't like it,' said Johnny. 'It's not what the school was founded for. It'll put me off my work.'

'Well, if you don't get into Oxford you'll have had a good term.'

Cigarettes cupped in hand to conceal the glow, the boys conversed quietly. The lights in the house behind them came on one by one. They could see the Horse's television flickering. In the other direction the lights of Bishopstown winked enticingly at the sea's edge.

To Johnny the idea of sharing the school with girls was disturbing since it involved an invasion of one half of his world by the other. Term was for friends and boys: holidays were for friends (different ones) and girls. In the holidays one met girls at point-to-points, partnered them at tennis parties and at dances, at the latter sometimes at excitingly close quarters. And he was undertaking a correspondence with Anne Bulow-Smith for whom a strong feeling had developed over the final week of the holidays, culminating in a visit to the cinema where they had leaned into each other and held hands. But this relationship would not interfere with any that might be developing at school. Similarly his attraction to David de Wet, who had only joined the school the previous term, had not in any way diminished his attachment to Anne. But how were things to be managed under the new regime? 'I mean, what are you supposed to do? Have two girlfriends – one at school and one at home? It doesn't make sense', Johnny lamented. Could he imagine standing in one of the back rows of the chapel next to Anne and watch out for David de Wet amongst the trebles at the same time? It was a confusion.

The first cigarette of the term was stubbed out in a mood of some apprehension.

❊ CHAPTER 2 ❊

The
Waggery

The mood in the Waggery was more militant, it being declared that the Wolf had gone too far. It was not the fact of girls they objected to but the fact of yet another innovation. What was happening to the old order when the Headmaster was introducing something new each term? Admittedly not all the innovations were unwelcome – for example, the greater freedom to go into Bishopstown – but what with monthly reports, house involvement in chapel services, the establishment of the tutorial system and so on, there was a sense of the school's true character fading rapidly away, leaving the boys with a life quite different from the one they had bargained for.

The Waggery was to the school what Nick's study was to the house: the social centre. It was one of those rooms that has had a hundred uses but never quite settled into one. Situated off the library, it had been, within Johnny's memory alone, the librarian's office and dump, a classroom and drama wardrobe. Its present function had been established by the Hawk, a new and young member of staff whose candidature for the role of girls' housemaster had been passed over on grounds of his lack of 'form'. Like the Burk he had enthusiasm but unlike the Burk he was not disliked for it, such was his good nature.

The Hawk was dedicated to the Arts with evangelical fervour

and to the development of a literary elite at Worthington. One of the means to this end as an extension to the Literary Society which he also ran was the establishment of the Waggery (a mildly facetious name of his own choosing) as a room in which certain favoured lights of the Upper School would gather informally for the mutually enriching exchange of intellectual talk. The wags, as members were termed, were elected by their own number and the officers were responsible for the room and the conduct of the wags. They were answerable then to The Hawk who, standing ostentatiously clear of his own creation, could not always resist the occasional visit to check on progress. On these visits he was sometimes disappointed, sometimes not. Members were allowed to work there during prep which was a valued privilege and the Hawk had installed a collection of modern works of literature – such names as Hemingway and Sartre, Lawrence and Nabakov featured – with which he hoped his pupils would become familiar. By such means they would qualify themselves for membership after school of an *avant garde* literary world – reviewing in small circulation poetry magazines, play-producing in the provinces etcetera – to which he himself had not quite the talent or the courage to aspire.

The evening had passed quite pleasantly. One of the wags had read titillating extracts from a recently published and much acclaimed novel which the Hawk had daringly bought for the Waggery that centred on the passion of a middle-aged man for a pre-pubescent girl. The wags were listening with suppressed avidity, puzzled by the remoteness of middle-age and the unattractiveness of pre-pubescent girls, but intrigued by the sexuality that was unquestionably passing along this improbable axis. Johnny had then done some work, his books open on the table, it being prep time, his huge lexicon propped up so as to conceal anything behind it if need be. In fact he'd made quite a good start with Euripides' Medea which the Burk had just begun with them as one of their A Level set texts.

Prep then over, it was time for one of the activities for which the Hawk had certainly not founded his progressive institution:

the preparation of the weekly Top Ten. Johnny himself could never be quite happy about this rather crude assembling of fleshly talent and was glad that David de Wet had so far been insufficiently attractive to make it on to the list. Nick's fag and Angus' crush, Luigi, had been hovering between one and three for two terms, though on this occasion one of the wags was arguing that a certain coarsening of feature was now taking place. There was always some instability about the first list of term, when boys' girlish good looks had, as with Luigi, changed and when the wags had not always quite got their eye in after an exclusively heterosexual holiday.

In the Waggery too, speculation about the Burk's likely involvement with the girl innovation was rife. This speculation – soon to take on the substance of a rumour before swiftly being known for a fact – had perhaps emanated from the sage reflections the evening before of Billy and Nick. Although those two were often voted into the Waggery neither had ever attended it, which perhaps enhanced their peculiar status. The Burk possibility had gripped the general imagination and lent added feelings of revulsion to the idea.

'The whole thing's ghastly.'

But grumbling was common and did not carry with it any consequence of resistance or remonstration, let alone rebellion. What was decreed was as inevitable as weather. It is true there had been the celebrated Kipper Rising, when one morning at breakfast every member of the school demanded his rightful fish, to the embarrassment of the catering staff who had been making a steady weekly reduction in the number of their dark and desiccated fillets on the grounds that hardly anyone wanted them. The Rising had been effectual and kippers came off the breakfast menu. But on the whole acceptance was the norm. 'Take all in patience' was the Chaucerian saw unknowingly inscribed in the heart of the Worthingtonian.

Johnny next contemplated writing to Anne but the mood wasn't right, not because she had been replaced in his fancy by young David de W but because... well, it had just sort of happened. In fact a kind of emotional lassitude had come over him. What was the matter? Was this normal? Was this what adolescence was – one minute burning with passion, the next bored out of your mind?

'Hey – Christ!' exclaimed one wag out of the blue, 'any of you lot seen the Hawk's wife?'

'The Hawk's wife? – didn't know he had one.'

'Married last holidays apparently. In the chapel.'

'Married in the chapel? What an obscene idea!'

'Anyway, what about her?'

'Bloody attractive.'

'Yeah?'

'Blonde, nice legs.'

'Christ!'

'Lucky bugger.'

'Can you imagine it?'

There was a short silence while the speakers attempted to do so. The Hawk – for all his artistic aspirations – was so breezy and tweedy, so ordinary and nice and unsexy, that it was not possible to imagine him engaged in any sexual activity, particularly not with a luscious blonde. Whatever else might be said about sex, Johnny concluded, it was a mystery, that was for sure.

The conversation developed fairly raucously along improper lines, then the Burk appeared. As someone who listened outside doors before entering he'd probably heard a fair amount of the conversation. However, although he was habitually severe on any form of disrespect or misbehaviour, he would not have been displeased by what he heard for it was at the expense of his rival, Mr Hawke. Enmity would not be the term to describe their relationship since the Hawk was incapable of ill-feeling but the Burk entertained for him the envy and ill-will that Iago has for Cassio. As a colleague and a Christian he could not allow this ill-will to find direct expression, so it was through third parties and his enemy's creations that the Burk was able to indulge his malice. Now of course, in addition to the existing grounds for hatred, was the possession of a beautiful wife.

'Are you looking for someone, sir?' a wag inquired in a tone poised expertly between politeness and insolence.

'Merely attracted,' came the oleaginous reply, 'or should I say 'distracted', since I was looking for a book in the library, by the sounds of culture.' The Burk stressed the final word with a complacent sneer. It was a pleasure to him when the schoolboy's natural propensity for ingratitude and the misuse of freedom was evident for it must serve to undermine the trust and confidence of those who granted it – in this case the Hawk who would one day realise the naïve error of his ways and learn the truth of the pedagogic adage: Trust them and they'll let you down. 'Are you quite fulfilling the aims of the founder in such behaviour, I wonder.' With which ambiguous remark he was about to leave when catching sight of Johnny he remarked, 'Wags have tutorials too, don't forget.' Then he left.

'Christ!' exclaimed Johnny. 'I had forgotten. Nine o'clock.'

The Burk, as a bachelor, lived in the Founder's Tower, a building of some five or six storeys given over to the accommodation of unmarried members of staff. A bedroom and sitting room, with a distant and shared bathroom comprised the quarters, the Burk's being on the top floor. There Johnny soon went, climbing its wooden staircase, a little uneasy, as ever, at the prospect of being alone with his tutor. The man sought to make you feel at ease and failed in doing so. There also lurked in the memory of anyone closeted with him the near-scandal concerning the legendary and now early-departed Robin Felton, a boy of such surpassing beauty that hardly anyone dared even speak to him. The Burk, thought to be as smitten as anyone by the boy's smooth-skinned appeal, took it upon himself in a fit of pastoral ardour to put him right in his behaviour, which he considered flirtatious and liable to undermine the moral rectitude of any young fellow susceptible to bodily charm. His manner in the interview – thus went the story – had become heated and his means of persuasion physical to the point at which the luckless and wholly innocent youth had contemplated escape out through the little panelled door that gave eventually on to the leads of the Founder's Tower, his nearest escape route. The scandal that might have attended this episode had it gone any further or the boy been vindictive would have been considerable. But it never reached officialdom and so remained part of popular legend by which the boys' lives and attitudes were unconsciously shaped. Thus, although Johnny ran no such risk as poor Felton, he was uneasy alone in the company of the man: there was something about him.

On the other hand, Johnny felt when he was actually with him that there was also some sort of vulnerability to him. To be sure, his exotic choice of tea was designed more to impress than to please but was there not something pitiful about the need to impress? There was truly some pathos underlying the man's unpleasant exterior and off-putting manner that Johnny, perhaps unconsciously trained to it by his rectory upbringing, could not but sense and respond to. ('People are not bad,' his father said, 'just weak.')

While the kettle boiled on the ring, the Burk led with the conventional conversational gambit – the holidays, a topic of little interest to any boy more than three hours into term.

'Any dances?' he enquired lightly. 'How's your quickstep – or is it something a little more modern nowadays? The rock-and-roll perhaps?' The Burk sought to project a self-image both ingratiatingly up-to-date and engagingly old-fashioned.

Johnny thought of the dimming of the lights during the last waltz at the Seymours' dance and blushed. Luckily the Burk was engaged with ladling Lapsang into a petite cane-handled tea pot and did not notice.

'I'm not a very good dancer, I'm afraid, sir.'

'Bad luck on your partner,' observed the Burk, not unkindly.

But there came upon Johnny the sudden apprehension that the man was going to lead the conversation into matters romantico-sexual in his role as moral tutor. Spurred by this anxiety, Johnny wished to divert such an embarrassment but the topic was compulsive. 'What do you think of the introduction of girls, sir?' he accordingly asked.

The Burk smiled wryly and turned the question. 'What do *you* think?'

'Well, I don't really know, sir. We'll have to see. It'll change the place a lot, won't it?'

'How do you think you will feel about sharing a classroom with members of the fair sex?'

'I suppose it'll be more like real life,' Johnny replied lamely.

'Oh yes,' said the Burk. 'Now, do you think it is warm enough to take tea on the roof? We can but essay. You haven't been up there, have you?' the Burk enquired breezily. Johnny, who did not relish heights nor confined spaces if his company was to be the Burk, replied that he hadn't. 'Then let's take tea with a view,' said the Burk as if offering a much sought-after entertainment.

So, each carrying his cup and saucer – the cup a small, oriental item without a handle – and his host a tin of French biscuits also, they made their way up on to the roof. This involved going down by way of a little stone passage, dark and dry, and through a sort of upper room with a wooden floor whose sloping timbers supported the leads of the tower roof itself. From this room a little low door gave on to the narrow space where one could stand with the security of the sloping roof leads behind, the chest-high stone parapet in front. This four-sided walkway, open to the heavens, afforded no sitting place, but in the south corner there was a slightly raised platform of hexagonal shape and about six feet in diameter. 'Perhaps they meant to build a turret on it,' the Burk thus accounted for it as he deposited cup and biscuit tin to hoist himself gaily up upon it without any regard for the fact that its outer edges had a parapet of barely two feet high. Johnny felt sick just to look at it and had hardly the stomach to get up on the platform at all. One side, however, had a high parapet and once upon the platform and with his back firmly clamped against this with legs outstretched, Johnny felt a little more secure than he had expected, particularly as his position was such that he had no sight of the ground below him but only of the view. He resisted a craven temptation to wrap an arm around the flagpole.

Built on a spur of the South Downs, the school enjoyed an unrivalled panorama. The view from the top of the Founder's Tower was spectacular – due south over the English Channel, east over the river valley to the string of seaside towns fringing the sea and north over the smoothly undulating Downs with glimpses of the Weald beyond. It was an unusually mild and still evening for early May and under its genial influence the Burk settled down to what he clearly intended should be a good pupil/teacher chat. Johnny, however, unaccustomed to his masters seeking to behave like humans, was on his guard.

'And what do your friends think of the idea?' the Burk enquired, pursuing the theme of the introduction of girls.

Johnny's 'friends', he knew, signified in the Burk's mind Billy and Nick, mainly the latter who had become his *bête noire*. It had been in class that they had first met and conflicted. Nick had been placed in one of the General Studies groups on classical antiquity which were conducted with enthusiasm by the Burk. At the time the crisis occurred these classes turned on archaeology, some of whose less spectacular finds were on display in showcases at the back of the Burk's classroom. The most knowledgeable and enthusiastic of archaeologists would have been hard put to it to breathe life into this jumble of dusty shards, each so small, dull and shapeless as not to begin to suggest the function or the beauty of the complete objects of which they were only pitiful fragments. The Burk, rashly attempting this task of imaginative recreation, could deal with the massive indifference of his pupils when it was accompanied by some small measure of dutiful compliance but Nick would not even rouse himself to get up and look at the cases on whose contents his teacher was so eagerly discoursing. Such plain insolence could not be let pass. Fired beyond reason by his own sense of social inferiority and professional and personal humiliation, the Burk launched himself upon this living rebuke to his own power and pride – and came off considerably the worse. Since then Nick had not attended his classes and the Burk lacked the courage to challenge his absence which he had not reported since he didn't want him back. This situation was agony to his soul.

What then did Nick think of the idea? The Burk fished slyly for some view that would confirm his distaste of its author and which he could viciously confute in the safety of Johnny's simple company. Johnny would not be drawn, however.

'I think they feel it'll be a lot more natural,' he replied, feebly coming up with a slight variation on his earlier reply.

'Ah yes, Nature,' replied the Burk, according the concept a capital letter. 'It is hardly natural for boys of your age particularly to live for long periods without the company of the opposite sex. It tends to put the members of that sex on a pedestal on which they may be adored in a dangerously idealising way or from which they may be pulled down by degradation. Sentimental idealisation or cynical sensuality: not a desirable dichotomy.'

Johnny felt out of his depth with this and had the uncomfortable feeling that they had fallen into the dreaded subject of sexual morality after all. He didn't know what to say. Staring through the battlements at the soft light on the Downs to the north, Johnny wished he were behind the raspberry canes having a fag with Angus. But the Burk had barely started.

'Nothing but evil comes of shielding the young from the truth of supposedly adult matters. Human sexuality does not commence on the receipt of an A Level certificate. It is no good leaving matters till then, there is plenty of scope for error before that time.' He faded momentarily at this and began to fish for his pipe. This object, in shape like the one favoured by the famous detective of Baker Street, was produced during periods of reflection or relaxation. It was clearly an affectation but it seemed to give him real pleasure too. 'In the old days,' he continued, tamping the contents of the capacious bowl with a pallid forefinger, 'it was thought proper to give dire warnings and no information. Hardly the best approach. I have long argued for the inclusion of sex education in the school curriculum.'

Oh God, thought Johnny, spare me! Was the Burk now going to launch into the details of what such a course might contain: vivid illustrations of the female anatomy, methods of contraception?

'Innocence is a fine thing,' he however went on in safely philosophical vein, 'but when the flames of passion burn ignorance is but tinder.' Taken by surprise and not a little pleased by this extemporaneous aphorism, suggested perhaps by the operation of lighting his pipe in the early stages of which fire predominated over smoke, the Burk paused to puff even more copiously, clouds of Virginia wafting gracefully upwards into the pale blue of the evening sky above them, like pedagogic prayers. 'Or as Hamlet expresses it,' he went on, drawing Shakespeare in as secondary support, ' ' Oaths are straw to the fire in the blood'. '

There followed more on this subject but Johnny felt, thinking about it as he made his grateful way at last down the oak staircase of the Founder's Tower, that it was all more for his own benefit than Johnny's – as if the man were practising answers for an interview. Well, it all amounted to further evidence of his being at least a candidate for the job of first girls' housemaster, this dwelling on the subject of sex. But was it right that it should figure so largely in his mind? And if he were talking of the need for sex education of the young what had his own youth been like? It was not possible to imagine the Burk as a schoolboy but he must have been seventeen once, like Johnny himself now, though of course being young was different in those days. Could he have had 'fire in the blood'? No, he was probably too busy digging up Roman remains. And now? Well, the Robin Felton incident showed that there was something at least smouldering still.

✳ CHAPTER 3 ✳

The
Literary Society

In the days that followed, ordinary days of lessons and school food, of cricket practices and cigarettes, there were no developments in the plan for the introduction of girls. The Burk was giving away no more of his own views on the subject of sex, much to Johnny's relief, and there was no further news to feed gossip on.

One of the highlights of the opening fortnight was the first meeting of the Literary Society. This, as has been mentioned, was organised by the Hawk and comprised some fifteen to twenty boys of literary interests, the members of the Waggery. That these wags were widely known as 'the shags' by the general populace only confirmed their sense of their own superiority. Hitherto, meetings had been held in the Hawk's room in the Founder's Tower. There a play or a paper would be read, coffee (on festal occasions, cider) would be drunk and biscuits (sometimes chocolate-coated) would be eaten. But now on his marriage the Hawk had moved to one of the suburban dwellings that housed married assistant masters. These, located on the outskirts of the school grounds, were to answer the needs of family life, and of a design suitable to the modest professional status of their occupants.

There the wags trooped one fine evening, their noisy progress cheered on by cries of 'Shag!' from study windows.

And there they were not to be disappointed in the Hawk's wife, whose beauty had been so glowingly reported .

Angus later claimed that he first saw her standing in the hall with the evening light behind her and shining through her diaphanous skirt in such a way as to outline her body beneath the waist in a way that combined revelation and concealment to a uniquely titillating degree. This sight, which Billy, who was reading Joyce, said should be termed an epiphany, came upon Angus with such force that he actually stumbled in the doorway on entering and had to be helped into the sitting-room, where he fed his eyes on the angelic vision the entire evening. Even Nick (who attended the Literary Society if not the Waggery) was visibly impressed, so that in her presence his customary ease and politeness with adults took on a part-respectful, part-flirtatious style. And when he rose to give her his seat on the sofa, perching on the arm himself, and to share with her his copy of the play to be read, it did not go unnoticed that his position afforded him an enviable angle of vision down the front of her dress, an angle down which his gentlemanly instincts could not entirely prevent his vision from sliding.

The Hawk was happy and all oblivious, and the evening passed for the wags in an atmosphere of electrical intensity. Mrs Hawke had not taken a part in the play, though requested to do so by her husband and the unheard prayers of the boys, on the grounds that one real female amongst a number of males reading female roles would merely be confusing. This view, expressed over the coffee and biscuits gracefully served by her at the end of the evening, naturally led to the topic of the introduction of girls into the school.

'Well, soon you won't have that problem, I gather,' Mrs Hawke added. There was a general rumour of assent amongst the sippers and scrunchers, though no specific conversational response. The Hawk was sitting back and puffing contentedly at his pipe, an object less absurd in design than the Burk's, pleased with his wife, the wags and the occasion. 'Any of you got sisters that might be joining you?' Mrs Hawke attempted brightly, with no better result.

'There will be the question of accommodation,' now put in Nick, who was really indifferent to the matter in itself but not willing to have Mrs Hawke lump him in with the rest of the gauche bunch who were then floundering conversationally in so shameful a manner.

'Yes,' said Mrs Hawke, 'they'll need something better than those dreadful barrack-room dormitories you boys have.' The image of this divine creature actually inside a school dormitory was unassimilable. 'But of course there will only be a few to begin with, I believe.' She turned to her husband. 'And didn't Derek say he had his eye on somewhere in the school, John?'

If the wags' sharpened intuition had not told them instantly that this was a clanger, that this light question was actually a brick of monumental proportions, one look at the Hawk's demeanour would have revealed it. The transformation from genial, paternal, pipe-smoking presider over a pleasant social occasion to a blushing stutterer was complete and near-instantaneous. The pipe was snatched from the mouth, the lounging posture became erect, the blood rushed to the face and there was a general moment of silent horror while the question hung with all its deadly lightness in the air.

The clanger was severalfold. For one thing, the use in front of boys of the Christian names of members of staff was unknown. That the staff had Christian names and what those names were was common knowledge to the boys – they even used them amongst themselves of more favoured masters – but one did not address one or refer to others by their Christian names, as the Hawk would, in an hour or so, be tactfully intimating to his luscious spouse

Now Derek being the name chosen by the Burkinshaw parents for their offspring, Mrs Hawke's question had revealed at a single stroke both that the Burk was indeed to be – as Billy and Nick had surmised – the master in charge of the girl operation and that he had already fixed his beady eye on some particular part of the school as the future (if only temporary) home of the first intake of girls. This could be anywhere, from a section of the study block, to the disused laundry, to the top floor of the Wolf's large house. But wherever it might be, the choice carried considerable political and practical implications which were far from ready for general publication.

In Mrs Hawke's innocent remark etiquette had been breached, confidentiality broken and a very large cat let out of the bag. The Hawk, red and sweating, mumbled something about prematurity and uncertainty at this stage and changed the subject. But the damage was done and it was in high spirits that the members of the Literary Society, taking a final hungry look at Mrs Hawke, stepped out into the night to make their way home.

'Let's go up to the Ring,' one suggested.

'No need, we can smoke here.'

But the decision was in favour of the Ring. This latter was a clump of trees on a shoulder of the Downs above the staff houses. Its association with the Iron Age or the Romans was of much less interest to members of the school than its convenience as a meeting place well away from the school. A curious local inhabitant having, however, indignantly delivered to the Headmaster's study door a sackful of empty bottles and cigarette packets, the Ring had been placed out of bounds. It was thus an ideal place to meet and there the Wags proceeded in order to have a cigarette and celebrate the riches of the evening. The twinkling lights of Bishopstown below harmonised with their mood and there was much capering and hilarity as a breeze off the sea tousled their hair and swept their voices inland.

The physical charms of Mrs Hawke were dwelt on at length and in detail though more with sentiment than lewdness and Angus was almost speechless with adoration. He drew thirstily on Nick's hip flask and his mood intensified to a near-explosive pitch. Soon the glowing ends were extinguished and the return home begun. They were late, but lawfully so, having attended a school society, as they would complacently inform the Creep, if that nocturnally vigilant member of staff happened to meet and challenge them.

'Well, you were right, Billy,' said Johnny. 'It is the Burk.'

'It's an appalling idea,' another wag opined. 'Appalling.'

'It seems odd, though, appointing a bachelor to look after girls,' said Nick. 'I mean, what will Mr and Mrs Bourgeois say at the thought of their daughter, hitherto cloistered securely in a remote rural nest of spinsters like St Agnes, being in the sole charge of an evil-looking and unmarried sod like the Burk ?'

'You know what – he'll have to get married.'

'Who to?'

A number of candidates for the part of Mrs Burkinshaw were canvassed, but, as already indicated, the field of femininity at Worthington was small.

The hedgerow glimmered richly white in the moonlight and the masses of may, now in full bloom, shone brilliantly. One wag who was reading Proust recalled Marcel's embracing of the pink hawthorn blossoms on Swann's Way and this prompted Angus, in a state of extreme stimulation by infatuation and whisky, to make a similar display of emotional transport. Plunging into the blooms with the purpose of taking them in his amorous arms he quickly recoiled with cries of pain as the unseen spikes of the shrub stuck into him. The general view was that this served him right.

Voices quieted as they approached the now darkened school buildings and the evening concluded without further incident, the wags dispersing to their several houses. Billy went to do some work but Angus, Johnny and Nick repaired to Nick's study where the attentive Luigi, long since gone to bed, had cleared up, leaving a fresh orange salad which the three consumed with relish. He had also left his Latin prep which Angus, his passion now running high in a quite different direction and his mind fuddled with drink, could only very perfunctorily complete. He soon after went to bed, having the First XI to represent the following day and left Johnny and Nick to a quiet chat.

Johnny was uneasy about the quality of his Virgil construe which none other than the Wolf, standing in for a temporarily absent member of staff, would be hearing the next morning. But it was too late to have another crack at it. He envied Nick who had got clear of the dead clasp of Latin and Greek after O Levels, and chosen those subjects that required little classwork – it was not only the Burk's lessons that Nick cut – a great deal of reading and the occasional writing of very long essays. Nick was not often to be seen at work but he claimed to do it all in the small hours. Johnny was not a small hours man, particularly not that night when, as he suddenly remembered, the next day was a saint's day and he was to be sacristan.

'Christ! it'll be seven o'bloody clock!' he lamented.

Dashing for cover from the rain into the chapel cloister at one minute to seven the next morning, Johnny found himself walking alongside the subject of the previous night's discussion, likewise headed for communion. The Burk was as cheery as the weather was foul and Johnny was sleepy. The cheeriness was appropriately transformed on entry into the crypt into a look of solemn piety that was maintained throughout the service. Johnny eyed him at prayer with growing distaste – the bald pate bowed and gleaming whitely, the thin pale fingers tufted with black hairs as thick as bristles. After chapel the Burk stepped briskly into the masters' dining room with the eager air of one who has earned his breakfast and can't wait to get at the day. Really, Johnny thought, it was one thing to be utterly disgusting but to be so cheerful with it was too much.

❊ CHAPTER 4 ❊

The Dance
Against St Agnes

The school dance, referred to in the Wolf's beginning-of-term speech as one of the liberating innovations of the era, was an annual fixture arranged with a 'sister' school not far distant. St Agnes, Chancton, belied its saintly name by an almost total want of spiritual ethos and academic prestige. It was regarded as a safe sort of school for not very bright girls whose principal interests were horses, parties and boys; those Worthingtonians who had attended previous dances – Johnny and co had not been hitherto eligible for the event – could warmly testify to those last two.

In the Waggery debate raged extensively on the subject of whether the dance should be attended.

'I think we should boycott it on political grounds.'

'Why?'

'It's all part of the co-educational plot.'

'But it's happened in previous years.'

'Maybe, but it's different now. Anyway, you know who's in charge, don't you?'

'The Burk.'

'Quite.'

That he had this role was of course yet more evidence (if such were needed) of the man's crucial involvement in the whole girls project. Behind another objection that dances were all very well in the holidays lay an unacknowledged sexual timidity on the part of the objector, although this was not unmixed with a reasonable disinclination to make the sexual *volte face* involved in suddenly, for one evening only, becoming heterosexual after spending several weeks in a homosexual environment.

Angus' attitude was straightforward: anything that conduced to the possibility of sexual or romantic experience was to be welcome. His new passion for Mrs Hawke must of course remain on the ideal level, along with his old crush on Luigi, whereas the dance might offer more tangible delights. Johnny himself was excited by his friend's expectations and could not resist the temptation to send home for his dinner jacket which he had only recently acquired. It included his pride, the pink velvet cummerbund which would, he trusted, go some way to compensate for the evidently second-hand condition of his DJ as well as what he considered his own lack of masculine charm. His mother dispatched the outfit promptly and with encouraging remarks.

By the evening of the dance itself there he was, cummerbunded and hair-greased for the first time in his life, in Angus' study, nervously drinking a cup of coffee.

'Oh, they'll go for that,' said Johnny, seeing Angus in his kilt.

'This is what they'll go for,' Angus replied, lifting the front of his kilt to reveal a fair-sized member amongst a mass of black curly hair.

'Christ! You're not going like that, are you – with no pants on? Supposing you fall over?'

'They'll love it!'

On further discussion, however, Angus decided on wearing a jock-strap, beginning to doubt – as his imagination moved further into the realms of sexual possibility – the power of his sporran to act as suppressant in the event of arousal.

'Shall we take fags?' Johnny wondered.

'Might be a search.'

'I can't go through this without a cigarette all bloody evening!' Johnny's nerves were getting the better of him.

'What are you getting so twitchy for? You've been to a dance before.'

'Yes, I know. I just get nervous.'

Later he put it down to premonition.

They both sprang to the window as a coach came up the drive and drew to a halt outside the dining hall. Lifting up the skirts of his kilt in an act of delighted self-exposure – though at the same time ensuring that there was no real danger of his being seen – Angus called, 'Come and get it, girls!' This act of sexual self-confidence on Angus' part, together with the spectacle of some three dozen tulled and chiffoned maidens, pink and blue, debouching with nervous excited chatter on to the parade ground, was almost too much for Johnny.

'It's going to be bloody,' he moaned.

But Angus soon had him in tow and downstairs so that they emerged from the house according to Angus' plan in time to fall in with the fluttering group picking its shrill and high-heeled way over the gravel. Their self-consciousness was too daunting for even Angus' confidence and he contented himself with walking alongside the group at a little distance and casting appraising glances at the company, not without the beginnings of reciprocal interest. It was actually Johnny who recovered his manners if not his confidence, to ask the mistress-in-charge if he might show them the way to Great Hall where the dance was to take place – there had, awkwardly, been no official welcoming party. The formidable lady in charge accepted with an uneasy smile and drew her hairy stole around her shoulders in a defensive gesture that implied a determination not to be disarmed by male flattery. She was accompanied in the role of protectress by a much younger person who was chatting with the girls behind. The modern style of her dress and the look in her eye suggested that she did not see her function that evening as entirely custodial.

They were soon met in the cloisters by the Burk with

apologies for not having greeted their arrival – the formidable lady had to admit they were early – and with no hint of recognition of Angus' and Johnny's hostly role in their visit thus far. The Burk, in his appearance, had surpassed in vulgarity the most uncharitable expectation. His dinner jacket was of ostentatiously modern cut, the satin lapels starting at the single centrally-placed button and, instead of terminating at button-hole level in a broad angular projection as in Johnny's double-breasted number, flowed on upwards, slimly and in an evenly curvaceous manner, right round the back of the neck. Under this, nestling on an evening shirt rich in lacy frill, was a modishly thin tie of such compact structure as only pre-manufacture could achieve. At least, Johnny reflected, the bastard hadn't got a pink cummerbund. The Burk attached himself to the youthful protectress as much as to the more senior female in charge and, glistening with self-approval, led them to Great Hall.

That lofty room had been decorated almost out of recognition by some Upper Sixth formers who were experienced in the trappings of such occasions. The venerable panelled walls were almost entirely covered with bunting and multi-coloured paper-chains. Balloons hung in generous bunches and the band, installed on the stage with their shining instruments, their natty dress and individual monogrammed music stands, had imported to the school an air of the glamorous and pleasurable aspects of adult life so markedly absent there. Great Hall had been transformed. Former headmasters with their severe clerical countenances hardly added to the gaiety of the scene but the frames of their portraits were brightly festooned. Tables of food and drink stood ready, behind them servers dressed in black with neat white aprons.

On the entry of the girls the young males in the room reacted like a herd of bullocks to an intrusive human. There was a spasm of movement, much of it backwards as some boys felt a sudden need to go and brush their hair or rehorizontalise a bow tie. Some stood still, staring dumbly at this novel spectacle and quite at a loss as to how to react. On the part of a few there was a very tentative step forwards. At that point it was hard to see how the evening could achieve the quality of social ease expected of it by its organisers. There was the Wolf shaking hands with the mistress of the mohair stole. The only conversation now was between members of the same sex as both halves of the company seemed quite paralysed by the sudden sense of occasion and its own air of expectancy.

It was the band that saved the situation by striking up some familiar tune to a rhythm that the body might respond to, so that there were soon couples on the floor and the evening was under way. The boys quickly grew accustomed to the grotesque spectacle of their masters – including the Horse and the Cow, and even the Creep – in evening wear and dancing. Soon some firm pairings of boy and girl were established. Angus and his partner danced as if they were childhood sweethearts. The injunction not to leave Great Hall in couples, together with the strongly non-alcoholic nature of the fruit cup, increased the latent sensuality of the occasion, a sensuality intensified by long deprivation. Having eased the evening into action, the band then moved into a programme that oscillated somewhat awkwardly between traditional dances like the quickstep and the waltz, whose movements only one or two of the young were confident in, and the cha-cha, whose movements only one or two members of staff had an idea of. During the former the younger generation either shuffled awkwardly about the floor, conscious of the cold sweat on their hands and the difficulty of conversation, or took the opportunity of inching their way breathlessly to closer physical contact with each other. During the latter the older generation made laughing and self-deprecating attempts to master the modern: a distressing spectacle.

The announcement of supper came to Johnny as a relief from the necessity of dancing, though he found himself attached to a girl called Sarah. She was rather short and spoke softly so that most of the time she was invisible as well as inaudible. He had tried to find her attractive but had not succeeded in doing so. During one dance, in an attempt to provoke a little discharge of sexual electricity, he'd made a mild thrusting gesture with his pink cummerbund which had just made contact with Sarah's torso at the level of the ribcage but it had evoked no answering movement on her part. Of her upper half he got a good bird's eye view but there was nothing much to it.

Over the chicken mayonnaise he encountered Angus who had clinched for himself the most flagrantly attractive female in the place. Angela had a blonde and sizeable lusciousness. Her rich hair flowed to her shoulders whose exposed skin had a natural, lightly tanned smoothness no cosmetic attentions could imitate or improve. The soft and fleshy warmth of her body radiated almost palpably into the atmosphere and that, together with the indefinable but unmistakable suggestion of physical availability, would have generated in any male a deep rumbling of lust. Johnny was dismayed more than anything by this unique blend of submission and provocativeness and Angus discreetly nudged him, patting his sporran with prurient complacency.

A quiet but deep desperation welled up in Johnny's soul. Shackled, apparently for the rest of the evening, to a girl with whom he had established no rapport and otherwise surrounded by females either equally unattractive or, in the Angela bracket, too attractive to contemplate, or already spoken for, he began to despair of his own maleness, his own self. Wolfing his fruit salad, he excused himself guiltily from little Sarah and made for the exit.

On what thin threads our fate depends! By what trivial chances are our destinies governed! To follow through his present intention Johnny would in a minute or two have been in his study throwing off his pink cummerbund, collecting the cigarettes with which to console himself in the bogs for the failure of his masculine aspirations, sinking with warmth and regret into the familiar bed of school, embracing by default the reassuring quotidianities of a life without passion. And it was simply a glance that changed it. Approaching the door, he happened to look towards the tables on his left where the dancers were still gathered. Behind the tables and dressed in the discreet black and white of their trade were two serving girls whom until then Johnny had not noticed. One of these was instantly recognisable as Tina the Tucker but it was the younger that arrested his attention now. Of moderate height and dark straight hair... but her features went unparticularised in Johnny's soul which, in catching sight of her, sprang to life with a celerity and fieriness of which he had not imagined it capable. 'The rich golden shaft' had penetrated. So astonishing was the vision, so richly composed of all the warmth and wealth and beauty that the world had to offer, Johnny was unable to move or stay, unable to understand how she could exist without bringing that world to a halt as having achieved in the supremacy of her beauty and loveliness the purpose for which God had created it. No need to enumerate her charms, to analyse the nature of her appeal. She was beauty, she was love, she was the embodiment of all he had ever yearned for, the drying of all the tears of childhood, the restoration of the lost Eden of his unremembered infancy, the fulfilment of the promise of an adult world of joy and a heaven of adoration beyond. She was his past, his future, his living present, a gift of God, the meaning of life. His love, now and for ever.

CHAPTER 5

After the Vision

For a long moment Johnny stood entranced. Then, coming to and realising how absurd he must look, he proceeded with his original intention of leaving the Hall, not to return that evening. Into the cloisters he stepped and walked alongside their familiar arches in the quiet evening. It being prep time, there was a stillness about the place, only the movement of his own dazzled and dazzling self as he floated in a new state of being. Two acquaintances, glimpsed through a window of the Waggery, had that unenviable mundaneness of the inhabitants of the mean suburban dwellings you pass on your train journey to exotic locations. Johnny was now of another world.

But he was seized with a sudden panic lest the vision had been an hallucination or was no longer available and so he turned and hurried back into Great Hall. Yes, she was still there, still – incredibly – engaged in the humble task of serving food and drink to his school-fellows; still, in every movement and from every angle, of unparalleled beauty. Incredibly too she seemed unaware of the passion of his gaze as he walked slowly past her. Anxiously, with one eye still on her, he searched the throng for someone he could tell, but neither Nick nor Billy were attending the dance and Angus was heavily engaged with the coarse and uninteresting Angela, as she now seemed to Johnny. Instead he turned back and approached his beloved's table, joining the small queue awaiting service at her hands. By the time his turn came he found no words other than a pitiful Thank-you, and scarcely glanced into her face as she offered him the glass of fruit cup. He turned away from her in anguish, as at a chance lost for ever, bitter at his own failure to exploit his opportunity and at his own pusillanimity and bitter at her failure to recognise his passion and therefore to place herself, with a few tender but unmistakable words, in his heart. Couldn't she *tell*?

As if drunk, he was scarcely aware of his surroundings. The band played and couples danced. A wag drew his attention to the Burk whose partnership with the girls' younger protectress had been virtually uninterrupted and to all appearances mutually pleasurable since their first encounter in the East Quad. Driven by the urgency to act and by a corresponding incapacity for action, Johnny roamed in desperation. He must speak to Angus – Angus would tell him what to do and lend him the confidence to do it, but where now was Angus? Johnny scanned the dance-floor, thronged with happy couples; he scanned the walls, thinner now with girls trying, though unpartnered, not to look left out and with boys, though unpartnered, to look manly; he scanned the food and drink tables – even catching sight once again of his beloved – but there was no sign of Angus and his blonde. More desperate now almost than at the possible loss of his love, and knowing the absurdly early hour of the dance's end to be fast approaching, Johnny dashed for an exit.

The interdiction on couples' leaving the Hall would, he knew, have little binding effect on Angus once his blood was roused. The numerous classrooms that lay nearby were scarcely conducive either to romance or to sex but they had the merit of being unlikely to be entered at any time during the evening by anyone in authority. This merit had attracted two smokers, Johnny discovered, as he flung doors open in his frantic search, but also the object of that search. Gazing hand-in-hand and somewhat improbably at a map of Ancient Greece, stood Angus and Angela. Perhaps cooled by their separation from the party and the unconviviality of their surroundings the couple had entered a phase of suspension, a sort of trance.

'Angus, can I see you a minute?'

'What?'

'I want to talk to you a minute. It's urgent.'

'Christ!'

Outside, Angela abandoned to a solo contemplation of Ancient Greece, Johnny explained. He did not attempt to do justice in his explanation to the depth of his feeling, but merely put the position. What should he do? Angus was in no mood – sullen as a man pulled back from the verge of sexual adventure – to enter into Johnny's feelings anyway, scarcely to consider his friend's plight.

'Go and ask her what her name is,' was his suggestion.

'I can't just go up to her and ask her that, can I?'

'Why not?'

'Well, it's bit direct, isn't it?'

'So what?'

'Well...'

'OK, be even more direct and ask her to dance.'

'Dance?! She's supposed to be serving.'

'Well, it's getting towards the end of the party. Anything goes. Who's going to stop you?'

'I suppose I could...'

'Of course you could,' Angus affirmed, reaching for the doorhandle of the classroom in which the object of his own amorous intentions might, through neglect, be cooling dangerously. 'Now bugger off, Johnny, I've got work to do. Good luck.'

With swift and determined tread Johnny now made his way back to the Hall, cutting an unseeing way through dancers and onlookers to the sacred corner of the room. But, alas, what a sight met his eyes! Stripped of their cloths, the trestle tables were bare except for a pile of cardboard boxes to take the glasses.

'Well, that's nearly that,' came then the voice of Tina the Tucker emerging from under one of the tables, shoving a box across the floor with her foot. 'How they expect us to have it all packed and done up and that, I don't know. Ten o'clock we were supposed to have finished and here it is gone quarter-past.'

'What about...' – for Johnny, although on the verge of despair, had seen a chance – 'what about your helper?'

'Oh, she's gone. Yeah, her dad come and collected her prompt at ten – well, she's not older than you are and with a day's school tomorrow it's only right she should be off in good time.'

'That's a pity for you,' Johnny gasped, unable to pursue the obvious.

'Yeah, she's a good girl, Jane, a good worker.'

Jane. Her name was Jane.

It had been offered to him without asking. The treasure was placed unsolicited in his hands. Johnny turned his gaze towards the dance floor. Now that she was gone he could relax, her image, her name captured firmly in his heart. The music had slowed and softened for the last waltz and though there would be no dimming of the lights a certain intent hush had fallen upon the dancers as most of the couples closed in while some held aloof from the physical intimacy in which Angus and Angela led the field. The Burk and his partner, it was widely noted, were not in the clinching category but there was no doubt in the minds of the onlookers that their hearts beat as one.

Jane.

Not for Johnny the gathering and goodbyeing, the couples wandering reluctantly off to the St Agnes coach. The experience was his own, not now to be shared by others. Company was out, bed was impossible. He set off alone up the Downs path out of school and towards the Ring. Safely distant, he lit a cigarette and ambled slowly over the open grassland, pausing from time to time to look back at the lights of

Bishopstown and the bright coastline to the east. Ahead of him lay the dark undulations of the Downs, above them a half moon doing duty in a clear sky. It being May, the sky was hardly quite dark though it was close on midnight. The day was reluctant to end and Johnny's spirit chimed with it.

Jane. Gradually, like the moon descending the skies, Johnny came down to earth a little. He then found, rather to his alarm, that he could not assemble Jane's features in his imagination. Her general appearance – the black and white – her figure, these were inescapably caught, but the exact configuration of her face eluded him. All he had, apart from the passion of his heart, was a vague image and a name. These might at first seem treasures enough to a man in love but where should he go from there? That she attended school, was about his age (or younger) and had a father were the only other scraps of information he had. Not very useful. However, he could deduce that to be free to attend an evening function meant day school which, in turn, meant living somewhere not too far away. That was good news, though for Johnny any distance – and here he made an unhappy survey of his vast horizons – was considerable, there being public transport only to Bishopstown.

What was the occupation of the father who had come to collect her so promptly? Why had he, Johnny, not asked Tina further questions? Well, all was not lost – he could quiz her at the Tucker the very next day. With this practical intention Johnny blew up the embers of his passion and walked slowly back to school. Still reluctant to turn in, he called at Nick's in case the latter was engaged in late night study and prepared for a beer and a chat. But there were no lights on and, rather puzzlingly, there was evidently – his bedroom door being open – no one in the bed. Nick had certainly not been at the dance so where had *he* got to?

This question was answered the following day when, in the morning break, Johnny called in for coffee to find Nick only just up.

'This is late, even for you, isn't it?' said Johnny a little grudgingly, having himself endured breakfast, chapel and three lessons, during the last of which he had passed the time toying with the letters J.A.N. and E.

'I was rather late last night,' Nick replied.

'I know. I called in around midnight,' said Johnny. 'What time did you get in? Where were you?'

But this was too pressing an approach for Nick who liked to divulge his own information in his own way and in his own time. 'How did the dance go? Happy partnerships?'

'Oh, all right,' said Johnny, evasively. Rather than tell his own tale – he too could be secretive – Johnny reported on Angus' amorous adventures and on the Burk's.

'So the Burk was there too, eh?' Nick seemed unduly interested. 'Of him now I have something to tell,' he added, smiling mysteriously.

'Oh?'

'Yes, but it deserves a better place and time than this.'

Angus then came in.

'Have you heard? Johnny's in love!' he instantly declared, oblivious of Johnny's embarrassment.

'Johnny – in love? Well, well. Who is she?'

'The St Agnes girls were too classy for him – he's fallen for one of the birds who did the food.'

'A serving-wench i'faith,' said Nick facetiously. 'Tell us more, Johnny.'

Johnny was both appalled at this vulgar and insensitive treatment of his lofty passion and pleased that it was acknowledged.

'Well, all I really know is that her name's Jane,' he replied shyly, astounded that he could pronounce the sacred name in the presence of others. 'I haven't actually met her,' he added, and it sounded pathetic.

'Ah, love at first sight,' said Nick. 'No doubt Angus will put his romantic experience at your disposal to further the relationship.'

And he did. Later that day at the nets, Angus and Johnny representing First and Second Elevens respectively, talked it over. It wasn't to be a one-sided arrangement, however, for Angus, though he was much the more competent in the practical field, was weak in less direct forms of communication. He had not forgotten how Johnny had nearly two years before when the need arose instructed him in the art of love letter-writing, Johnny himself having been instructed by a precocious friend at home in the gradations of 'Dear', 'My Dear', 'My Dearest', 'Darling' etcetera. Now, with the return to their rural retreat of the St Agnes girls, Angus was obliged to pursue his amour on a more spiritual level than that in operation at the dance. Here Johnny would be helpful, the more so as Angus was not at all sure, now that the object of his attentions was gone, what his feelings for her really were. Limited opportunity had prompted instant action and that was gratifying, but the embrace quickly entered into was as quickly broken and it was not clear what basis, if any, to the relationship there now was. Had it just been what he called 'a one-night stand'?

So while padding up and waiting to bowl, it was agreed between them that Johnny would draft a letter to Angela on Angus' behalf and Angus would reciprocate with a direct enquiry of Tina Tucker about Jane.

The next afternoon therefore saw them in Angus' study looking out on a drizzly cricket-less afternoon and ready to exchange. Johnny had penned an affectionate and friendly letter to Angela which began 'My Dear', but this modest declaration could be made bolder in his next letter, he reassured the anxious Angus who was keen to pile it on in the interests of keeping the girl warm for their next encounter, whenever and wherever that might be. He had also concluded simply with a new item in his dictionary of epistolary lovemaking – the word 'Love' ringed in hearts drawn in red pencil.

'Bloody marvellous, Johnny,' Angus was impressed.

'There's nothing wrong with my imagination,' Johnny replied. 'It's doing things I'm not so hot at.'

'Well, talking of doing things,' said Angus. 'I've got what I can out of Tina about your Jane.'

'Yeah?' Johnny tried not to sound too eager. 'And?'

'She lives at Bockington. Know it?'

'Rings a vague bell.'

'Village about five miles north, got a nice pub. Her old man runs the pub, supplies the school with drink.'

'A pub!'

'Yup. Well, she was sort of serving behind the bar at the dance, wasn't she? She's not going to be the daughter of a stockbroker like Angela, is she?'

'No, I suppose not.'

'And she goes to the High School in Bishopstown.'

Johnny reflected for the first time on Jane's social position. Serving alongside the likes of Tina, father a publican, going to a state school – this was all a bit dubious. Then he realised he hadn't actually heard her speak: supposing she had an accent like Tina! Surely it wasn't possible that she could look so beautiful and sound so dreadful. But then would it really matter if she did? Would he not love her all the same?

'I think I know the pub, though,' Angus was saying. 'My parents took me there one exeat. At the foot of the Downs, got a garden and a stream running through. Quite nice.'

'You don't remember the landlord?'

' 'fraid not.'

'Anything else Tina say about her?'

'Not really. Just said she was a nice girl.'

'It's not much to go on, is it?'

'No, since you haven't even met her, it's not.'

'How would you go about it, Angus, if you were me? I mean, trying to get to meet her?'

Angus looked doubtful. 'Go to the pub, I suppose. Hope her old man lets you in. Hope she works there. Get chatting to her.'

The distance of the place and the difficulty of getting there plunged Johnny into despair. 'Maybe she'll come to some other function at school,' he said. This thought gave the hope of progress without the necessity of action and that appealed to him. 'It means waiting, though, doesn't it? Maybe I could follow her one day after school.'

'You could always write to her, I suppose,' suggested Angus. 'You're good at letters.'

' 'Dear Jane, You don't know me but I saw you at the dance the other day and I was wondering... ' Come off it!'

The grey drizzly afternoon contrasted horribly with the bright evening of only two days before when the St Agnes girls had stepped out of their coach while Jane – little did he know it – was already on school premises and it was only an hour or two before his life was to be changed for ever. And yet was it really changed?

'Hey, isn't that the Burk's car?' queried Angus, peering down the drive at a disappearing vehicle. 'Off to St Agnes to see Miss Whatshername, I expect. Lucky bugger.'

❊ CHAPTER 6 ❊

An Outing

'It's obviously made you both bloody miserable, you two –
falling in love,' commented Nick a few days later as both
Johnny and Angus sat glumly in his study.

'It's a bourgeois delusion, love,' was Billy's comment from
the chesterfield. He didn't raise his eyes from the book he was
reading. 'Stick to sex.'

'I try to', said Angus, 'but I find myself falling in love with
them as well.'

'Bloody miserable,' Nick repeated, regarding his friends with
paternal affection. 'I think we need an outing.'

This sounded promising, an 'outing' in Nick's parlance
signifying anything from an afternoon at the races, to a
nightclub in London, to a simple dinner or show in
Bishopstown. On one 'outing' they had been taken by taxi to a
scenic point on the Downs where, by prior arrangement with
his suppliers (Luigi's father), Nick had laid out a substantial
picnic. It was tacitly understood that the expenses of all such
outings were largely borne by Nick, though one would be
expected to place one's own bets or stand a round of drinks.

'I've arranged with David' – their Head of House:
conscientious but compliant – 'that we shall not be missed on
Thursday evening. If you two' – meaning Angus and Johnny –
'can have dental appointments or similar we can get away at two

o'clock. We'd better go by bus rather than taxi – it attracts attention.'

It was another part of the appeal of these outings that Nick always seemed to have every aspect of the arrangements – including the disciplinary – in hand. One was not only paid for but swept along without the necessity of decision-making and with little fear of being caught doing something one shouldn't that lurked so close to the surface of every aspect of school life.

In the event Johnny and Angus were delayed by cricket but by half past three, with arrangements to meet Billy and Nick who had left earlier, they were happily installed at the front of the top deck of the Bishopstown bus, cheerful at the prospect of that good town that offered so much by way of entertainment to the cloistered student.

A week since Johnny's first fateful sighting of Jane had been followed by no development towards any relationship. While Angus had already received a warm, if barely literate, response to his professionally composed letter to Angela, Johnny had done not a thing to make his beloved even aware of his existence, let alone his interest. Nonetheless Jane's image burned still in his heart: he imagined her all day long; imagined her as she was at the dance; imagined the words he might have said there; imagined how a meaningful look and an extended hand on his part would have drawn her, wordlessly but compulsively, from her menial labours out on to the dance floor, where, his left and her right hands clasped together, his right hand and her left respectively round slender waist and manly shoulder, they would have moved in harmony to the love-inducing strains of the last waltz. There a wordless communion would have united them to the depth of their souls. To imagine her outside that context was nearly impossible: her serving customers at the pub; her sitting at the breakfast table with her parents – he simply could not visualize the scene or believe its reality. Even less could he imagine her the schoolgirl, crouched over a Bunsen burner or chatting to her schoolfriends in the playground. At which apt point in his reflections he was disturbed by the familiar tone of lewd excitement in Angus' voice:

'Hey, there might be some talent here,' he was saying, leering out of the window ahead at the prospect of flocks of schoolgirls debouching through the school gates on to the pavement. It took Johnny a long moment to focus on the significance of this and of the sign 'Bishopstown High School for Girls' that they were passing.

'Johnny my boy,' said Angus, 'wake up – this here's your Jane's school, isn't it?'

Johnny was suddenly galvanized and leapt to his feet. 'We must get off here – I might see her.'

'Get off?! There's a hundred of them queuing to get on the bus. This deck'll be crawling with them in a minute. We wouldn't want to miss that!'

'But she won't be getting on it,' Johnny had already worked out. 'This bus is going into town – she won't be going that way.'

He scanned every face, however, that scrambled on as he and Angus pushed their way downstairs through the chattering, giggling horde on its way upstairs. The lower deck was full too as they gained the platform at last and so leapt on to the pavement only just in time before the bus lumbered on its way again. Johnny had glimpsed barely a dozen faces on that lower deck but then why should that bother him when he had already decided she wouldn't be on it – except maybe she would have to take a bus into the bus station in the town centre before catching her own bus out to Bockington. Perhaps he wouldn't recognize her anyway for she would be looking quite different in her schoolgirl's uniform and there was that frustrating problem of his inability to form a complete image of her in his mind, or even to visualize her features individually. He had got her nose for a while during an Ovid unseen and there had been a whole day when he had the line of her eyebrows but these details were fragmentary as well as transitory. Surely though, he reassured himself, when I do see her again I shall recognize her as strongly and certainly as on that first sighting.

Not on that bus, not awaiting the next, not chatting in groups on the pavement, not off on a bike. But she could have disappeared already – some girls had obviously gone before the bus arrived. The feeble hope that she might be among the straggling few still coming out of school held him there – Angus meanwhile as smug in the girlish throng as a pike tickled by minnows – though in a mood of growing hopelessness. Once the name 'Jane' sounded from one of the gaggles on the pavement and Johnny spun round but to no avail. Gradually the numbers thinned, groups broke up, individuals moved off. Members of staff, clutching capacious bags, hurried out, casting suspicious glances at the two youths whose unmistakable uniforms declared their membership of that elevated but untrustworthy establishment on the Downs. A caretaker could be seen, swinging a bunch of keys impatiently.

'No go?' enquired Angus not unsympathetically now that his own source of interest was dispersed.

'I'm beginning to wonder whether she actually exists,' replied Johnny dolefully.

'Don't be daft. Anyway, we can soon deal with that one. Er… excuse me… ' – Angus had turned to one of the few remaining girls who was evidently awaiting collection. Johnny stepped anxiously out of earshot but Angus was soon at his side again, steering him off along the pavement, headed for the town centre. 'Yes, she does exist. She's in 5A and you didn't see her this afternoon because she's away at a netball match. So.'

'Thanks, Angus,' said Johnny humbly.

'Try here again another day, eh?' suggested his friend.

'I can't just walk up to one girl in a mob of a hundred and say, 'Hello, Jane, you don't know me but I'm in love with you and my name's Johnny – let's go and have a cup of coffee. By the way can I hold your hand?' '

'Of course you can't, but you can watch her, see where she goes or which bus she catches. Maybe she does go to a coffee bar – you go in too and get chatting – you know, pick her up just like anyone else, all ever so natural.'

'You'll come with me?'

'Of course.'

Johnny cheered up a bit. Angus' plans of action always made their success sound virtually certain. They entered the material delights of town in high spirits.

At the appointed hour they rendezvoused with Nick and Billy at the back-street pub known to generations of Worthingtonians as safely indifferent to regulations regarding drinking age and unlikely to attract the patronage of any member of the College staff. Billy, a colourful exotic concoction held to his lips, was absorbed in the perusal of one of the books that formed a small part of his huge mound of purchases (for he too, like Nick, was possessed of great wealth). Nick, pulling nonchalantly on his Balkan Sobranie, was chatting up the barmaid, at ease in this modest public house as he was in any establishment that served the needs of the pleasure-seeker, be it restaurant, theatre, hotel or club.

The sad tale of Johnny and the unencounterable Jane was told before they gave themselves freely to the delights of the town. An extensive and varied meal at a Chinese restaurant followed the early evening drink.

'OK, Nick,' said Angus, 'now what's this about the Burk? Cough up.'

While his guests regaled themselves on the huge mounds of sweet-and-sour pork, bean shoots etc. that Nick had laid before them he regaled them with this other, anecdotal, fare.

'I went up to London on the night of the dance. It seemed a good opportunity – less likely to be noticed. Went to the club.' (Little more was known of Nick's family than that both his parents were dead – hence his wealth – and that a young uncle was a guardian. It was this uncle's club that was here referred to.) 'After dinner I went into the bog – one of those great marble temples of plumbing, you know, with brass pipes everywhere, beautifully polished. In comes one of the other members, old bugger – they're mostly old – and hoves to at the urinal next to mine... starts up a conversation: 'Evening off from school, eh?' 'Yes, sir.' 'Eton?' Well, I wasn't inclined to give the truth when being quizzed in such an impertinent manner so I replied, 'Yes.' 'Who's yer tutor?' he asks. 'Burkinshaw', I reply. Well, at that point the old bugger looks quite interested; up till then he'd just been making conversation to pass the incredibly long time it seems to take these old sods to have a pee. 'Burkinshaw, eh? I knew a Burkinshaw in the schoolmastering business,' he goes on. 'He didn't go to Eton, though – don't think they'd have wanted him at Eton.' And then the old boy goes on to talk about how he was a governor at... ' – here Nick named some public school of middling status in the north – 'and apparently this Burkinshaw got into some sort of bother.' 'Clobbering the boys, was he, sir?' I ventured. 'No trouble with boys,' the old sod said, and then he got all secretive and wouldn't be any more specific. Anyway this spot of bother was enough to make the governors feel that though it wasn't a sacking offence the Burk should move on – hence his appearing at Worthington. No scandal, no shame attached – just a different job in a different part of the country. But that's ancient history – must have been fifteen years ago or more, the old boy finished up.'

'Do you think the Wolf knows about that?'

'He wasn't headmaster at the time of his appointment.'

' 'No trouble with boys' – it suggests the trouble was with girls.'

'Well, if it was and the Wolf did know about it he certainly wouldn't be putting the Burk in charge of this new girl business, would he?'

'The Burk? – girl trouble!' Angus was indignant at the very idea. 'The only trouble he can have had with girls is getting anywhere near them.'

'He didn't do too badly at the dance, did he?'

'That poor woman didn't have anyone else to dance with, did she? Even the Burk's better than nothing.'

Speculation continued. Although the evidence was distinctly secondhand, remote and insubstantial there was general agreement that there might well be something in it. The thought that the Burk had some skeleton in his cupboard was very exciting to the company and put them in high spirits for the next part of the evening's amusement – the cinema. It was over choice of film that differences of taste amongst the company often generated dissension. Nick did not much mind what he saw but Billy had a strong predilection for recherché black-and-white Italian films with subtitles in which, though they usually concluded with several violent deaths in open-topped sports cars, very little actually happened other than that beautiful young men and women of the Maserati class hung around gravel pits at dawn in evening clothes saying little, doing less and generally despairing of finding spiritual significance in post-war European society. This confirmed Billy, whose country of origin in Africa had recently got out from under the British imperial heel, in his conviction of the collapse of the capitalist West and the rise of his own continent whose hour had at last come. The other members of the company found little relish in such intellectual entertainment and on this occasion the less artistic inclinations of Angus and Johnny prevailed so that they all went to see a recently released American film of which they knew nothing but which turned out to be just suited to their emotionally heightened mood.

The action took place in an establishment evidently commonplace in the USA: the summer camp. This institution seemed to be a kind of re-creation of school but on more relaxed lines and operating during the summer holidays. Boys and girls gathered – apparently of their own free will – to do things like play baseball, sing hymns and find places in which to neck. After the first five minutes Billy pronounced the film 'sentimental bourgeois rubbish' and recommended reading by the dim light of the Exit sign, but Angus and Johnny were enthralled by the beauty of the young heroine whose hair shone like gold and the romantic pathos of the lovers' situation. There were emotionally lurid flashbacks featuring a mother perpetually in trousers and perpetually drinking who gave her daughter (the heroine) a very hard time. There was a catchy and moving theme tune and some tender scenes in a loft containing fishing nets. Thus finding an emotional focus for his passion, Johnny was quite transported and wandered away from the cinema like one drunk. He could have walked to Bockington there and then or cat-burglared his way into 5A's classroom at the High School to leave a declaration of love for Jane on the blackboard. It was, however, now rather late and they must return to school.

Standing at the bus stop in a light drizzle with the prospect of being back at school in twenty minutes created a gloomy atmosphere.

'I hate climbing in,' said Angus.

'And we'll have to watch out for the Creep,' cautioned Johnny.

Only Nick remained equable; he had raised the umbrella without which he rarely left school and which he made no effort to extend beyond his own person. Billy lit up, not offering one to anyone else and retired into himself. Immediately behind them was a pub. Their ears picked up the chat and the clinking of glasses and it wasn't long before they were inside just in time for 'Last orders'. Nick, looking nineteen and with his red bow tie on, placed their orders while the others arranged who would keep an eye out for the bus.

How was it that the arrangement didn't work? – that a few minutes later they saw to their horror the upper deck of their bus pull past the window, leaving them stranded? The cheeriness of the pub had trapped them into missing the last bus home.

'Shit!'

Now as they stood at the bus stop, it was not just natural gloom at the close of a fine evening, it was the beginning of panic.

'Bloody hell!'

'Oh fuck!'

The casual obscenities and blasphemies in such common use suddenly took on the accents of desperation.

'What would Holden Caulfield do?'

'Take a taxi.'

'That's right – come on, we can get a taxi.'

But it turned out that they had not collectively enough money for such an extravagance. Nobody quite liked to hint at Nick's cheque book which had already done such sterling work through the evening. The local taxi drivers were anyway known for their greed, dishonesty and tendency to inform (after they had taken his money) on anyone from the College they encountered in suspicious circumstances. The boys ambled slowly down the street, trying to solve their problem; at least the drizzle had now stopped.

'What about walking back?'

This suggestion was met with withering silence.

'Any more bright ideas?'

'Steal a car.'

'Right, all those in favour of appearing in a magistrates' court as well as being expelled raise their left leg.'

' ' The situation appeared desperate for the four lads from Worthington, out at midnight on an illicit trip to Bishopstown with hardly a penny between them. How could they get back to school before dawn?' This was Johnny, transported into a whimsical monologue by the conflicting emotions of the evening. ' 'Was it the Wolf's study at eight a.m. and the old eight thirty-eight to Victoria with the bags packed and an inferior position with corresponding salary and poor prospects in Uncle Bill's solicitor's firm in Croydon? Or would they be set upon in a dark alley by a gang of youths to be found the next day weltering in their own gore, the luckless victims of class warfare reminiscent of – ? '

'Stop your bloody weltering, Johnny, Nick's thinking.'

Nick was standing still, apparently contemplating a garage

door. Only it wasn't an ordinary garage door – it was a fire station door.

'Ooh, brilliant idea – we're going to steal a fire engine.'

'Do you realise,' Nick began in didactic tones, 'that should there be a fire these doors would burst open and that that red monster there would shoot out' – and he thrust his now furled umbrella dramatically – 'and make top speed to the conflagration?'

'That is what the lads with the little choppers are paid to do, yes.'

'Which means,' Nick continued, rising slightly on his toes in order the better to peer in at the gleaming red-and-silver, beladdered monster within – 'which means that should a fire alarm sound forth from the sacred precincts of Worthington College this very machine will whisk itself there, lights flashing, bells ringing, in a trice. I think, therefore, that we will now have a fire at Worthington and that present company will return to school by fire engine.'

❊ CHAPTER 7 ❊

A Ride on
a Fire Engine

Angus was the first to find his tongue at this proposal. 'In other words,' he said tentatively, 'how handy it would be if the old school burned down. Right?'

'That's the idea,' put in Johnny sardonically, 'we kneel on the pavement here and pray that at this very moment some member of the school is seized with a fit of arsonism.'

'Pretty long odds on that,' said Angus.

'Oh ye of little faith,' Nick intoned, 'how much longer must I be with you?' And so saying he pointed his umbrella: at the corner of the street stood a telephone kiosk. He said no more.

'Dial 999!'

'And ask for Fire – tell them the College is ablaze – brilliant!'

'Do you really mean... get a lift with the firemen? They'd never take us on – not just like that.'

'We will secrete ourselves about the vehicle,' Nick replied calmly.

There was a moment's silence while faith and doubt fought it out in the collective breast of the company. They were helpless in this dire situation of being out of bounds and with no means of getting back to school, a situation that could have serious disciplinary consequences, and they were as dependent on Nick's savoir faire to save them as they had been on his cheque book to entertain them. The trouble was his proposed means of rescue seemed likely to entail even worse disciplinary consequences. Offending against school rules was one thing but breaking the law was another. Before this inner fight was resolved, however, they were distracted by the appearance near them of a disreputable-looking character in an old coat. He was slow and unsteady, blatantly drunk. The tramp was discoursing incoherently to the vacant air with many gestures.

Nick spoke with sudden urgency. 'Billy – to the phone – dial 999 – ask for Fire – to Worthington – quick.' Billy obeyed.

' 'It is an Ancient Mariner

And he stoppeth one of three,' Nick intoned loudly as the tramp came more or less level with them. So dramatic was this declaration and accompanied by so bold a gesture with the umbrella that it penetrated the consciousness of the lurching inebriate, though it would anyway have been difficult for the man to avoid him since Nick had courageously grasped him by the elbow to be sure of detaining him. The man, turning a bearded visage and an unfocused gaze in the direction of his sudden and unexplained companion, was entirely non-plussed by this poetic salutation and stood silent and swaying in Nick's power.

'Bloody hell, Nick, what are you doing? Are we taking him on the bloody fire engine as well?'

'He serves our plan, dolt.' Nick was now offering his companion a cigarette – an offer that had a powerful capacity to concentrate the hazy attention of its beneficiary, as was intended. Being a Balkan Sobranie, the cigarette was blue, but if this curious contrast with the shade commonly associated with such a thing confused the man he overcame his confusion sufficiently to steady himself and aim a hand at the proffered object. 'We stay here,' Nick continued, adroitly applying his lighter flame to the shaking cigarette between the man's lips, 'we stay here until the fire engine is about to emerge. Our friend... ' – who at that moment burst into a fit of coughing – 'our friend here will be the cause of the engine's delay long enough for us to board it.'

So saying, Nick courteously invited the tramp to join him on the damp tarmac forecourt of the fire station. This invitation, at first holding little attraction for the man, absorbed, after his fit of coughing, in the pleasure of an unusual smoke, was reinforced by the offer of the hip flask and he was soon squatting on the ground, Nick companionably crouched beside him. Billy then returned from the telephone kiosk.

'Well?' Johnny enquired.

'I think we should see some action,' Billy replied calmly. 'The only problem was that I had to give them a name and where exactly I was calling from.'

'And you said… ?'

'I said my name was – '

At that moment the building behind them sprang into life: a bell started clanging urgently upstairs while downstairs, where the fire engines were, a bright light came on.

'Nick, for God's sake – what are we doing?' The others were desperate for instruction and Nick appeared to be in happy conversation with his now nearly prostrate companion. Inside the fire station shouting and more clanging could be heard, then – fearfully – the roaring into life of a powerful engine.

'Nick!'

In a moment Nick had joined them at the very doors, abandoning his hip flask to the tramp who had returned to an upright position to give its little remaining contents his fullest attention. Next the doors – or rather one set of them, for there were two – rumbled loudly open and the company backed themselves up against the dark of the unopened ones as the fire engine, with a brilliance of head lamps and a preliminary clang or two of its automatic bell, sprang forth from its lair – only, of course, to come to an immediate halt on the forecourt at the back of a tippling vagrant bang in its way.

What was said to the boys' unwitting accomplice in their escapade or how the firemen handled him out of their urgent path of course the boys never knew, being engaged during those vital seconds in clambering on board the engine.

Everyone knows what a fire engine looks like but not everyone would be capable of taking up a position on one that was safe, let alone comfortable. It was necessary to make for the back in order to avoid being seen by any of the firemen using either door at the front. It was something like getting on to a small yacht – most surfaces seemed to be irregular, there were unexplained hooks and knobs and brackets and stanchions, but there were also small flat areas and shelves where a foothold could be gained. In the end – by the time the engine resumed its urgent way, leaving a bodily-transferred and bemused tramp on the pavement – the company had succeeded in finding hand-and-foot hold in the area of the ladder turntable.

It being a late weekday evening there was little traffic, and the fire engine sped – though with more noise than speed – through the streets of Bishopstown on its life- and property-saving mission. Nick, characteristically, soon found a place to sit down in tolerable comfort and, drawing his coat about him against the air that proved chilling at that speed, contemplated the retreating lights of the town with the quiet equanimity of a tourist on the upper deck of a lake pleasure steamer.

'Not a view I've ever enjoyed before,' he mused.

'What if the police spot us?' enquired Angus anxiously. No one replied.

'Billy, what were you saying the problem was,' Johnny shouted over his shoulder, 'about ringing 999 and having to give your name?'

Billy had been anxious for his parcel but having settled it in a small compartment of no apparent function he wore, if not the relaxed air of Nick, then the slightly bored and uncomfortable look of a strap-hanger in a crowded tube.

'Oh yes, my name. Well, I told them my name was Burkinshaw and I was calling from the Founder's Tower.'

'Burkinshaw!'

'I had to give them some name. But I didn't attempt to imitate the voice.'

'Terrific! So when they've actually located the Founder's

Tower and not discovered a fire they'll be looking for the Burk –'

' – who'll be reading Plato in his pyjamas in front of the gas fire in his room. Great!'

This ridiculous image suddenly turned their earlier anxiety to excitement, and the fear of consequences melted as they sped along. Johnny began to sing the theme song from the film they had just seen, while Nick declaimed one of the stirring exhortations of the Aeneid, while Angus embarked upon a foolhardy mounting of the turntable ladder round whose base they were situated. His declared intention was to proceed the full length of the ladder which overhung the windscreen of the machine, and so to offer the driver and those seated in the front, the amazing spectacle of the sudden suspension of an inverted face. From getting very far with this rash exploit he was prevented by the tight grasp of Billy and the dismissive voice of Nick who drew attention to the dangers of more blatant public exposure. As to their being exposed anyway, they were not observed by any police. If anyone else noticed the curiosity of four youths unofficially attached to the rear end of a fire engine, they did not, either then or later, draw anyone else's attention to it. In fact, Bishopstown slipped away without incident and they were soon approaching school.

'Hey, are we going all the way to the Founder's Tower on this thing?' Johnny enquired anxiously.

'No,' replied Nick, ' it'll slow down as it turns in at the drive – we'll get off there.'

The fire engine did more than slow down at the entrance to the school – it came to a virtual standstill, there being quite an incline as well as a sharp turn at that point, so that the boys were able to get off without danger and one of the college servants, returning from late-night duty in the masters' dining room to his humble quarters in the erstwhile gatekeeper's lodge, saw no more than a fire engine, properly manned and equipped, proceeding up the drive towards the main buildings of the school.

The last the boys saw of their transport was it rounding a

distant bend in the drive as it slowly ascended on its errand of mercy.

'The sky is not exactly livid with flames and the stars blotted out with smoke, are they?' observed Billy laconically as they quietly took the back path to school.

'Let's nip up there and see what happens,' suggested Angus. 'I'd love to get a glimpse of the Burk being hosed down in his pyjamas.'

'Better not,' Nick soberly replied. 'I think the time has come for a discreet withdrawal.'

And so they went to bed: Nick to the quiet slumbers of a general after a successful battle; Billy to the sudden awkward remembrance that he had left his parcel of books on the fire engine; Angus to a mental replay of the exhilarating ride which would pad out a letter to Angela very nicely; and Johnny, both to the agony of being so near Jane at the High School that afternoon and the bliss of the emotional transports triggered by the film whose heart-stirring theme tune, revolving in his head, played him softly to sleep.

Derek Burkinshaw was indeed in his pyjamas and preparing for bed at just the time the fire engine arrived. In fact he was taking his customary ten draughts of fresh night air from the window when he heard the unusual sound of a powerfully-engined machine coming to a halt on the scrunchy gravel of the Founder's quadrangle. Whatever might be the occasion of it was more the night porter's concern than his but natural curiosity and the over-scrupulous sense of responsibility that afflicts many schoolmasters, drove him, in his dressing gown, to the head of the stairs. If at that point there seemed anything to investigate he would investigate it. He then heard heavy boots on the stairs. This hobnailed tread had the unhurried quality of a fireman who is now sure that he has been the victim of a hoax but whose duty requires some investigation of the situation, if only to impress on as many minds as possible the severity of calling out a rescue service without due cause.

To Derek Burkinshaw, however, standing on the top landing in all the vulnerability of pyjamas and dressing-gown, the ascending boots had a menacing quality and his bold and conscientious intentions turned into nervous apprehensions. Avenging angels, skeletons leaping out of cupboards and chickens coming home to roost stirred in the recesses of his psyche and converted the workmanlike clomp of heavy protective footwear into the jackboots of a recriminatory agency bent on night arrest. Guilt and fear sprang in Derek Burkinshaw's heart and he was about to make a sudden withdrawal into his room when adult sense reasserted itself and he was ready to confront whomever now approached him so unusually shod.

The midnight conversation that followed between a fireman in full equipment and a schoolmaster in pyjamas established that though the latter was indeed Mr Burkinshaw, he himself had made no such emergency call as had brought about this situation. He promised to investigate the matter, however, as it did seem likely that the hoax had originated in the school and – yes – he agreed, such behaviour bordered on the criminal, the fireman's lot could not always be a happy one. Thus mollified, the fire captain went on his way down the stairs to his patient colleagues and their redundant engine. The sound of retreating boots sent balm through Derek Burkinshaw's spirit and he returned to his room with a sense of a job well done. He congratulated himself on the mature blend of calm, efficiency and tact with which he had dealt with the situation – headmasterly qualities, he reflected complacently, though berating himself for having failed to introduce a judiciously humorous note at some point and to round the whole with an offer of refreshment. Then he heard the boots returning. Going to meet them this time more with curiosity than apprehension, he was presented by the fireman with a paper parcel of books that had inexplicably been found on the machine. 'You might find these some help with your investigations,' the fire captain said. 'Goodnight.'

Mr Burkinshaw, once more alone, examined this piece of evidence with fear and distaste. The contents varied. There was a volume or two of unexceptionable material – the inspiring purple colour of a certain paperback company's way of designating work of Latin or Roman origin. But there was other matter less reassuring – works by writers who combined intellectual respectability – sometimes even Nobel laurels – with the most irregular and subversive ideas on Judaeo-Christian religion and morality and western civilisation in general. The portrait photographs of these authors, who all looked hunted, offensive, dissipated, French or were smoking, taunted Derek Burkinshaw with the simplicity of his bourgeois philosophy and way of life. Gingerly turning these books over, as if they might contaminate him or perhaps bear valuable fingerprints, and glancing again out of his rooftop window over the innocently slumbering school, he began to speculate.

The hope that these volumes had been inadvertently left on his own machine by a fireman of unexpectedly intellectual interests and anarchistic tendencies could not be reasonably entertained for long. Nor would such an explanation of them account for the hoax fire alarm in his name. That had been a deliberate act – mischievous or malicious – and must be confronted as such. There were one or two youngsters amongst his colleagues in the Common Room who might have been tempted to tweak his mortarboard but they certainly would not stoop to such a dubious and illegal prank. The puzzle of the possible connection between the hoax and the books, which were certainly of an adult nature, was not immediately soluble and he was obliged to go to bed with the uncomfortable conclusion that a member of the school had perpetrated an unpleasant joke against him and that there really was very little he could do about it for all his reassuring talk to the fireman about investigations. As to more precisely who might have been responsible he had his suspicions and those suspicions did not exclude at least two of the four members of the school so recently returned there by unorthodox means and now innocently slumbering. Oh yes, he had his suspicions, all right.

His own slumber, however, was troubled by vague but disturbing dreams of alarm.

❊ CHAPTER 8 ❊

Having
a Field Day

B ut as time passed the perpetrators of the hoax seemed to have got away with it. The story of the night arrival of the fire engine was the talk of the school for a day or so but the Burk was keeping his own counsel and the wags their heads down.

One early evening soon afterwards Nick and Johnny were enjoying a cigarette – or in Nick's case a cigarette and a drink – in the balmy sunshine of Nick's garden. 'Garden' was a grandiose term for a small patch of rough grass behind a hedge that ran alongside the back path to the school. Facetiously (and somewhat to Johnny's discomfort) Nick called it Gethsemane. In an earlier age this and neighbouring gardens had been cultivated as 'potagers' by the college servants who lived in the main buildings in small garret rooms since converted to dormitories. This 'garden' had many advantages: its short distance from the college buildings; thick conifers en route to it providing shelter from both rain and prying eyes; its concealment by a hedge; and its view, for it abutted on to a field that sloped away, giving an enormous vista to the coast and far out to sea.

'Fish-and-chip shops, factories and flats,' said Nick, sighing affectedly. 'What have we English made of our beautiful coastline? It's a tragedy.'

'Could be worse,' said Johnny. He rather enjoyed the scene.
'How?'
'Have a motorway built through the Downs.' (The M1 from London to Birmingham had recently been opened).

Nick shuddered. In his Noel Coward paisley dressing-gown and cigarette holder he was at his most languid, lounging along a bench that had earlier in the term and under cover of darkness been removed from the First Eleven cricket pitch boundary. It was softened with cushions. Johnny, sitting on the ground, felt at his most inferior to Nick when in this mood. In fact he often wondered why Nick seemed happy to spend so much time with him. He, Johnny, no great shakes at anything after all and the son of a home-counties parson was an unlikely chum for a rich, precocious and upper-class sophisticate. Why, Johnny had once asked him, had he come to Worthington when his forebears had all attended the famous establishment near Windsor assumed by the old sod at the club to be his alma mater? It was due to his mother, Nick had explained, who, following his father's untimely death, fell heavily under the influence of her local vicar who had recommended Worthington as being on the soundest of high church principles and best fitted to equip him for the moral challenges of life. She had died in a car accident – the family history was littered with disasters and premature demise – but Nick was already at Worthington and it was too late for his more worldly and traditional guardian (the young uncle) to move him. Unfortunately for his mother's religious ambitions, her son was completely impervious to the school's spiritual influence, at an early stage adopting the standard 'bolshy' school attitude in chapel of sitting when he should be kneeling and standing with his hands in his pockets when he should be holding a book and singing. The ancient and glorious liturgy, rich in music and language, the soaring nave of the loftiest school chapel in the country, touched him not in the slightest: he let it all wash over him. Nick was equally indifferent to the moral example embedded in religion, regarding morality as a middle-class invention with no claim on his conduct.

Although he envied his friend's free spirit, Johnny, in contrast, took seriously the religion in which he had been brought up and felt uncomfortable with his friend's unquestioning atheism. Nevertheless, friends he and Nick seemed to be.

'Going on Field Day?' Johnny now enquired. Silly question. Though Nick was nominally a member of the Corps (as all were) he was rarely seen in uniform and would certainly not have been induced to join others in wandering all day over the Downs with an old map, an incomprehensible compass, an inedible packed lunch, an obsolete rifle and a round of blanks.

'Alas, a previous engagement. I shall be in town.'

'Again!'

'My dear Johnny, it's my lifeline. I'm dying in this place. But if you're going on Field Day perhaps you'd like to borrow my gun.'

'I think we get provided with those, actually,' Johnny replied, taking Nick to be referring to the twelve-bore he kept under the bed. Though Nick was understood to have a house in the country as well as in town he was not really a sportsman (in the gentleman's sense) but had at an earlier stage in his school career persuaded the authorities that a little rough shooting with a neighbouring farmer was an acceptable substitute for football on November afternoons.

'I will be going to the Isle of Wight, though,' said Johnny, reluctant to be thought a complete stick-in-the-mud. Such a destination was hardly in competition with the Cote d'Azur and other chic overseas resorts favoured by Nick but it was as near to 'abroad' as Johnny had yet to go. It hardly required cholera injections – not even a passport was necessary – but it did involve a Channel (well, Solent) crossing.

'What on earth for?'

'Game of cricket. School where Kenny went to be head. Remember?'

'Oh yes.' Nick did recall a Mr Kendal who had taught German and surprisingly taken the post of head of a rather progressive school in a rather unprogressive part of the British Isles. 'I say, guess what,' Nick added with sudden vivacity, obviously changing the subject. ' Guess who I caught prowling round my flat yesterday.'

'The Creep.'

'No – Mr Burkinshaw. And d'you know what I'm thinking? I'm thinking – ' and here Nick was obliged to break off at the sound of voices and footsteps on the path behind them. Passers-by were rare and posed little danger, the hedge provided so thick a screen, but the path was occasionally used by members of the school, including staff. It was also a public footpath. This awkward fact was exploited by some of the young locals, tempted from time to time to poke the sleeping dog of the traditionally stand-offish (not to say inharmonious) relationship between town and gown. This evening's party had the accents of the town but it was neither large nor bent on trouble. All the same Nick judiciously remained silent while they moved on uphill. A louder cry from their direction a little later suggested that some minor provocation had been offered, though whether by home or away team it was impossible to tell.

Nick sighed dismissively by way of comment on this interruption and resumed. 'As I was saying, what I'm thinking is that Mr Derek Burkinshaw is sniffing out my quarters as a possible location for his girls.'

'Could be,' said Johnny. 'But they're not going to be needed for a whole year – they'll see your time out.'

'Possibly. But there may be a plan to put the school workmen in well in advance to bring the place up to a standard fit for human habitation. God knows it falls far short at present – the dump's terrible – they'll have to spend thousands on it. Then where shall I go?' Nick made it sound as if he were to be ejected on to the street and Johnny thought he was fussing but didn't say so.

'And what progress,' Nick now enquired, 'on your private life?'

Johnny was embarrassed, for what did his 'private life'

amount to? A strong but abstract passion for a girl, seen once, never met: a name, a school, a home – a face that his imagination could not even reconstruct.

'Loitering outside the school gates would certainly be undignified,' said Nick as they contemplated the options for action on Johnny's part.

'I couldn't write – just out of the blue,' said Johnny. 'It would be pathetic.'

'I think you need to find out more about her first, and then decide what action to take.'

Good old Nick, Johnny thought, trudging off to prep with at least some sort of next step suggested, though as his hour of Greek Unseen trailed slowly on he more and more wondered how on earth he should go about going about it.

Field Day opened unpromisingly with a chilly drizzle suitable to November. Soon after breakfast, however, skies cleared and the school was abuzz with preparations: members of the naval section, their Wednesday afternoon activity normally confined to learning knots in a classroom, were getting ready for a visit to Portsmouth where they would see – and possibly sail in – a ship; members of the RAF section, their corresponding activity normally confined to staring at a wingless glider housed in a remote shed, were off to an RAF station where they would see – and possibly fly in – an aeroplane. No such treat, however, awaited the greater number who were members of the army section. They might at some point enjoy transport by genuine army lorry but otherwise they would be putting their boots to the test in time-honoured fashion: a route march, of which the only good thing that could be said was that at least it wasn't square-bashing. The only consolation was that for the purposes of their allotted exercise they were issued with six blank bullets each since the route march had a destination and purpose: the assault and capture of a held position. This issue was only ever made on Field Day and was accompanied by a ritual of stern recording on clipboards and dire injunctions regarding their safe and sensible use. Popular mythology contained tales of some of the improper purposes to which the blanks had been put in previous years. These included the blowing-up of a grass-snake at very close range and the lighting of a cigarette. Today's recipients took possession of the blanks, eager to extend the range of such illicit functions.

'OK you lot,' said the boy officer in charge of Johnny's small platoon, aiming with these words at a tone blending casual good humour with underlying authority, 'over here. This is what we're doing.'

His men, with exaggerated reluctance, groaning and giving the odd Heil Hitler salute, rose to their feet from the wall of the armoury against which they had been getting themselves comfortable while their leader collected his orders inside, and clustered round him. Sergeant Frost – or Erf, as his men addressed him, that being his nickname – had little standing in the school, although an Upper Sixth Former. He was not even a house prefect and had obtained prominence only in the CCF, a common area of preferment for the conformist and the stupid.

'Bloody hell. We're not walking all that way, are we, Erf?' expostulated one of his men when the day's march had been outlined. The members of this platoon, with the exception of Johnny, a Corporal, were relatively senior in age but had attained no rank on account of a complete indifference to the means of gaining it: 'the awkward squad', as the CSM called them.

'We get the lorry back,' said Erf.

'Yeah, if it turns up.'

'And doesn't break down.' (Both these reservations were based on previous experience.)

'Stop grumbling and go and collect the packed lunches, one of you,' said Sergeant Frost, still keen to impress his authority on his men. No one volunteered for the task. 'Harrison,' then Frost ordered, choosing about the only one in his platoon he could be at all confident would obey him. Harrison duly slouched off to the back of the dining hall on his errand.

The mention of packed lunches had elicited a groan from the platoon members, such was the reputation of the College kitchen department's pre-packed meals. These – as their sobriquet 'sludge-bags' suggested – were mostly bread and/or pastry with little flavour and less freshness, most commonly a round of sandwiches and a slice of dry fruit-cake; occasionally a small wrapped chocolate biscuit; rarely fruit; never an accompanying drink, which the boys were expected to supply themselves. That such fare would comprise their sole refreshment until their return to school for supper confirmed the grumpy mood of Erf's anyway recalcitrant platoon as it shuffled off in the direction of the Downs, rifles at the trail.

They had barely passed the Ring when it became apparent to the members of the platoon that they were in for an appalling time. The day that had started so chill, damp and dull had rapidly turned into one of those rare May days when a burgeoning sun overwhelms a northerly wind to generate scorching conditions. Although the celandine was still yellow under the hedgerows and the cow parsley was yet to flower and the ash tree was still not in leaf, it was suddenly summer. The battledresses they had gladly put on over their scratchy shirts in a chilly dawn were stripped off, but had to be carried or tied by the arms round the waist, generating intense heat in the nether regions and worsening the discomfort of the coarse army trousers stuffed into gaiters at the ankle. Berets were snatched off and stuffed under shoulderstraps. Their clumsy boots were not designed for long-distance walking and there were complaints of blisters. These conditions were of course made worse by those compelled to carry the knapsacks of rations, the knapsacks being, like all army equipment, designed entirely without regard to convenience.

And then there were the rifles. Of course the boys were accustomed to these, going through the proper motions with them on parade, stripping them down, cleaning them and reassembling them, even marching with them, for short distances anyway. But now that they had to be carried for miles they became unmanageable encumbrances: unprovided with slings they could not be slung; shouldered, they quickly became uncomfortable at any angle; trailed, they became a dead weight.

So the beauties of the scene and of the day were more than lost on them. Indeed, they became aggravating factors, for the wide and rolling spaces that opened before them here at the heart of the Downs where the young green corn blades twitched in the sun and the larks rose at their feet was to them a barren landscape that offered only huge distances of flinty track down which they were condemned to trudge and the blue vault of heaven blessing them from above was the lair of a mercilessly sweltering sun and a burning wind.

After an hour they took their first stop in the shade of a corrugated barn beside the track. Its contents of straw provided some comfort as they flopped down, dropping or yanking off whatever they could.

'How much bloody further, Erf?'

Sergeant Frost, valiantly sustaining standards of appearance and attitude for the sake of morale, was hunched over the map which he had almost constantly been consulting as they walked. He was now at work with the compass. 'I reckon we've done about a quarter of the way.'

'Oh God!'

'Maybe a bit more.'

'Buggeroo. What do we do when we get there anyway?'

'Take a farm building. It's in enemy hands.'

'And do we have a plan of attack?'

'Not yet. I shall make one.'

'Bloody hell!'

They resumed their march. And the day got hotter and their blisters became worse and morale collapsed completely. Their first hour, as Johnny now looked back on it, seemed a carefree morning saunter compared with the endless painful trudging that had become a condition of life, a kind of hell that was without comfort or remission and could only become yet more agonizing and relentless.

'What about some lunch, Erf?' one voice demanded, though it was really drink for which they pined. At their last stop one of them had produced a small bottle of water that he had prudently brought with him. This had been requisitioned immediately on its appearance and swiftly dispatched by those who could get their hands on it. A quarter of a pint of tepid tap-water between eight gasping soldiers served only to drive them near-frantic with thirst. But on the Downs there was nothing but puddle water and the contents of the cattle trough, both rejected on health grounds. Perhaps, however, there might be some moisture in the contents of the sludge-bags: perhaps this year a tomato might have been included in the contents. Well, at least there would be flavour of a sort and appetites began to sharpen at the prospect of this much relief.

'OK, dish 'em out,' commanded Erf as they collapsed on a bank beneath a small clump of hawthorn, and the rations were unpacked. For the first time spirits lifted, if only a little. They must by now surely have covered most of their allotted miles – there couldn't be still all that far to go – and the prospect of food was heartening.

But fate would have it otherwise.

'Oh no – I don't believe it!' This from the unpacker of the knapsacks.

'What?'

'I don't believe it!'

'*What?*'

'They're... they're all... ' – the unpacker ripped at one after another of the paper bags... snatching at their contents, eventually holding up to the incredulous and horrified gaze of all the company the source and object of his own horror: a school pork pie.

The Worthington pork pie – the staple item in the sludge-bag – was an object of universal derision and disgust. The dark brown, dry and flavourless pastry on the outside gave way inside to another layer the colour of porridge, dense and slimy. The contents of the pie, which occupied less than half the space afforded by this farinaceous shell, was an agglomeration of pinky-grey nuggets of gristle overlaid with beige jelly. If the meat put on Pip's plate at that fateful *Great Expectations* Christmas dinner was in Dickens' words derived from 'those parts of the animal that the pig had during its lifetime least cause to be vain' the meat content of a Worthington pork pie was derived from those parts of the pig that the animal had, during its lifetime, been blissfully unaware of, so remote, internal and of so lowly a function were they. It was uneatable.

'Pies!'

'Nothing but fucking pies!'

There they lay, strewn upon the bank, all the bags ripped open to reveal that their sole contents were indeed the fucking pork pies.

'I'll bloody kill you for this, Harrison, you cretin!'

'Wasn't my fault – this is what they gave me.'

That one of the dimmer employees in the school kitchens, assigned the dawn task of preparing the picnic rations, had made a monumental error of distribution; that there were, even now, other platoons dotted elsewhere settling down on the sward in eager expectation of well-merited refreshment only to find that their sole portion was fruit-cake sufficient for a regiment – or nothing but cheese sandwiches or (less unluckily) chocolate biscuits; that such and such was the case was of no interest to the men of Sergeant Frost's miserable platoon who, their rising appetites thwarted, their thirsts torturous, now fell back into a torpor of despair.

Nothing but fucking pork pies.

❃ CHAPTER 9 ❃

A Significant
Meeting

And there was more bad news. He didn't know how to
say it but confess it he must: Erf had taken them off
course and they were still far from their appointed
destination, the farm building in a combe that had to be
wrested from enemy hands. They had walked the number of
miles expected of them, but had, alas, because of their leader's
error, two to go.

'I'm not walking another bloody mile, let alone another
bloody two miles,' was a characteristically mutinous comment.

While the platoon sprawled in such ease of body and mind
as could be achieved in the present lamentable circumstances,
and the luckless Erf pondered how on earth he was ever to get
his men on to their feet again, Johnny removed boots and socks
to stroll over the springy turf for a little solitary enjoyment of
the beauties of the day. Seeing a partridge pedal away into the
long grass he followed, hoping to find its nest. He had not gone
far, however, before the vista to which they had become
accustomed of ever-rolling fields and winding chalky tracks gave
way to a different view. Johnny found himself standing on the
edge of an escarpment, the ground at his feet dropping away to
the more level and wooded terrain of the Weald to the north.
Below him, to right and left, was a winding road, and
immediately beneath him, at the foot of a narrow wooded

combe, was a village. He was about to head back to his fellows to share this cheering information with them – for where there was a village there must be drinkable liquid of a sort, perhaps even a shop. God ! had anyone thought to bring any money? – he hadn't. He was about to run back when he identified, by the sign hanging at its door, the building right below him as a pub. No doubt about it: there was a car park and a little garden with wooden benches under the trees, and wasn't that a stream running down alongside it?

Within minutes of hearing this wonderful news, the revitalised cadets were quickly putting on boots, picking up rifles and eagerly stepping out. Some started chucking the hated pork pies over the edge of the escarpment into the trees beneath but the officer-in-charge, his sense of authority renewed by this hopeful turn of events, put a stop to such indiscipline. Very soon the men, rapidly negotiating the steep path downhill, arrived, panting and sweating, at their oasis. It was no mirage. It was a pub. There was indeed a stream. There were indeed tables beneath the ash trees through whose yet-leafless branches the sun threw its brilliance. And what the proprietor's daughter first saw as she helped her mother prepare food in the kitchen was what appeared to be a company of young soldiers lying on their stomachs drinking from the stream the cold clear water that sprang from the foot of the Downs above.

Beside the road the stream was channelled into a trough. Into this they plunged their hot heads up to the neck, and bathed their blistered feet in the stream. Their first and more pressing needs answered, the question of food arose.

'Anyone got any money?' enquired Erf.

Someone reluctantly offered up a half-crown. A miracle of loaves-and-fishes proportions being required, it was with little hope in his heart of adequately feeding his followers that Erf entered the door of the pub, clutching the requisitioned coin. It was a while before he re-emerged but his men were not impatient: there was still the present miracle of cool water to be enjoyed.

None of them would have believed that any circumstances could have rendered the sight of the ridiculous Erf welcome but when he did reappear he represented a miraculous vision, for he was carrying a tray on which were four pints of shandy. Immediately behind him came another figure, a man with a second tray similarly freighted.

'Here we are, chaps,' said the latter in cheery tones, placing his blessed offering on the table before their incredulous eyes. 'This is better than that water, I can tell you – looks clean but it's full of sheep's piss – get this lot inside you while we see what we can do about something to eat.' With a comic blend of gratitude and greed the boys fell on the drinks. 'I gather you've done some mileage and still have a battle to fight. Well, as they say, an army marches on its stomach so let's see what we can do. Won't be long.' And the speaker – evidently the publican – returned indoors.

The first thing to do was take a long, long pull. The second was to ask Erf, 'All this for half a crown?' Maybe he wasn't such a wreck after all. Erf explained that their host had taken pity on their situation and would be delighted to help – hence the drink and food. He'd been in the army himself, he knew what those bloody boots were like, he'd carried a rifle for miles and anything in his power he could do to ease their burden he would do. That's what he'd said, Erf reported, glowing with self-satisfaction at having pulled off this coup and rescued himself from the contempt and recriminations of his mutinous men.

Bloody marvellous, that shandy. What followed was better, for soon the first plates of food appeared, each covered in ham and chicken with salad and a huge chunk of bread and butter. While the first two lucky ones tucked in unceremoniously to this wondrous repast delivered in friendly manner by the proprietor's wife, Johnny fixed his eye on the door from the kitchen from which the next batch would come. One of the more self-possessed of the boys thanked their hostess for all her trouble and generosity. 'It's a pleasure,' she replied, 'we're glad to do it. And of course,' she added archly, 'you can always recommend the Rose and Crown at Bockington to your friends and relatives.'

The Rose and Crown at Bockington! Wasn't that... ? – and even as the fact dawned on his slow mind Johnny was visited by the vision for which he would gladly have crawled four miles and more to see, the vision that his pining soul had treasured with such desperate longing ever since that first sighting at the St Agnes dance. Out of the kitchen door, bearing a plate in each hand, stepped Jane. Heat, exhaustion, the shandy – Johnny nearly fainted at the sight, as the object of his devotion walked modestly across the car park. Those features that his struggling imagination had so failed to reassemble in his mind's eye were now before him in all their unique and stunning beauty, framed by the black hair. The blood drained from Johnny's face and then, as she arrived at the table and looked about to see who was still without food, it flooded back in. He blushed at his own blushing, was desperate to catch her eye, desperate that she shouldn't see him blushing when she would be bound – wouldn't she? – to know why and so to think how silly he was. 'One for you?' she said and he was obliged to look her in the eye. She leaned forward, their eyes met, she glanced down again, smiling slightly, turned and walked back to the kitchen.

Not shy, not forward. Demure and beautiful – oh, so beautiful! In taking the plate, Johnny had seen her hand close-up, had almost touched her fingers. And now here before him was the plate she had herself handled, with food on it that she had probably herself prepared. He would be putting into his mouth lettuce that had been in contact with her fingers! He didn't dare touch it. Around him the other boys were heads down and chewing. Ignorant pigs! Hadn't they seen what he had seen? There had been a vision, a visitation, and they munched on regardless. 'I'll have yours if you don't want it, Johnny,' said his neighbour with his mouth full.

But Johnny tucked in. He knew better than to draw attention to himself, still less draw attention to Jane. As it was, he might have to listen later to comments like, 'That girl at the pub was a bit of all right,' or worse, and he couldn't bear the thought. Besides he was hungry. She came back once more to deliver two more plates and Johnny gazed at her cautiously with voracious eyes. When she had disappeared back into the kitchen he had to begin to think. Being in transports of devotion was all very well but it didn't get you any further forward. Now it was unthinkable that having been blessed with a second vision he should not avail himself of the kindness of fate and seize his chance to make her acquaintance. It was perhaps now or never: it must be now. But what was he to do? Supposing she didn't reappear and they had to go? Supposing she had to go before they did? With these thoughts Johnny's adoring trance was quickly converted into panic. What the hell should he do? What would Angus do?

Then their host, who had introduced himself as Donald Baxter, came out again with a further supply of shandy 'to wash down the meat and make way for the pudding,' as he put it. He was soon in happy conversation with Erf, the map spread before them, discussing how they might go about the crucial phase of the day's intended action. Johnny saw his chance. Quickly piling two or three empty plates together, he set off across the car park, legs shaking with fatigue and dread, in the direction of the kitchen. By chance Jane was coming out of it at that moment and they met halfway. She held out her hands for the plates he was carrying, took them with a smile and a 'thank you' and returned inside, leaving him standing there. Lacking the courage to pursue her, Johnny returned to their table and there, his determination reasserting itself, picked up more plates and headed once more for the kitchen.

Determination rewarded. There she was at the sink, staring vacantly out of the window, the fingers of one hand held loosely under the hot tap in preparation for the washing up.

'Shall I put these... ?'

'Oh, thank you... yes. I'll take them. You needn't... '

Johnny spotted a tea towel. 'Can I give you a hand with the

washing up – I mean drying up?'

'Oh, no, don't bother. I mean… sorry, I don't mean I don't want – '

'I'm pretty good at it,' he said, sort of laughing. 'I do it at home. Hopeless at washing, though,' he added, picking up the tea towel. It was a somewhat frayed object with a design of sealyhams on it but Johnny considered it easily one of the most beautiful things he had ever held. She seemed reluctant to look at him, intent on the washing up. 'Very nice lunch,' Johnny said to her silent profile protected from his gaze by a curtain of that unbelievable dark hair. It was straight but came down in a swooping sort of way and curled up and forwards a bit at the end, like a hook. Not having to look her in the eye gave him courage.

'But you haven't finished yet,' she said, quickly turning and flashing a smiling face at him that nearly slammed him against the opposite wall.

'Oh, I know, I can see that.'

'No, no, I don't mean that… ' – she was flustered – 'I don't mean the washing up,' she said, again looking at him but only quickly and was she blushing too? 'I mean the lunch. There's the apple crumble to come yet. In fact I can't think why I'm doing this – I ought to be taking that out to… '

'It's all right, I'll do that,' said her mother, coming into the kitchen at just that moment. 'You carry on with the washing up, Jane – particularly as you've got a helper' – she smiled at Johnny – 'still, I don't suppose you have to do much of this at your school, do you?'

'No,' Johnny replied. 'No, we – '

'He does it at home, though,' said Jane, her back to them both.

Her mother paused, looking with interest at Johnny. 'Does he now?'

The rest of the day was an absolute bloody triumph. After their lunch, the platoon, now in a state of contentment as deep as their despondency had been earlier, bundled into the hospitable Mr Baxter's Dormobile.

'Twelve years old, done sixty-five thousand miles,' he said proudly.

Though it had little power and was weighed down by a payload of nine people it accommodated them all (if not comfortably) and transported them (if not swiftly) to a convenient spot from which to launch their scheduled offensive. Donald Baxter and Sergeant Frost were as excited as each other in their tactical planning and the Dormobile came in handy in distributing individual members of the attacking force at different points so as to effect a complete surrounding of the farm building under siege. The attack was synchronised and complete surprise achieved against a force demoralised by boredom and the consumption of cheese sandwiches without other refreshment. The *coup de grâce* was delivered in the form of a bayonet attack, pork pies substituting for actual bayonets in a dramatic manner for, impaled upon the ends of the rifles, they exploded on discharge of a blank round into a gratifying shrapnel of pastry and gristle before which the enemy was helpless. The victory was total.

Or was it? Erf's men, pretending to head, like the defeated platoon, for the rendezvous point where the army lorry was due to collect them for return to school, actually rendezvoused with the Dormobile, in which Mr Baxter took them back to Worthington. So at supper that evening there were two platoons in contrasting mood: Erf's with its military victory, full stomachs, refreshed by a late afternoon shower or swim, their blisters having been ministered to by kind Mrs Baxter; and the opposition, defeated and ill fed, who had returned, owing to the predictable unreliability of the army lorry, only a minute or two before supper itself. The anecdotal good humour of the former group with tales of shandy, unauthorised transport and misused blanks which spread rapidly, enlarging as they went, contrasted with the bitterness of the latter. The leader of that defeated platoon decided to give an account of the day's events to the Commanding Officer of the CCF, a man with a strong sense of discipline and fair play, confident that some retribution might follow and his men be avenged. Erf had led his platoon more by good luck than good judgment and he made a poor job of defending himself and his men against the charges; fatigues were the consequence.

❊ CHAPTER 10 ❊

An Exchange
of Letters

Well, who cared about a few silly fatigues when he had Jane to think about?

Again and again Johnny replayed in his mind that little scene in the pub kitchen with Jane at the sink, him and the tea towel with the faded pictures of the sealyhams on it, what she said, what he said. The big question was: did she by any remote chance have anything like the same interest in him as he in her? Well, for a start, why should she? Just as the rest of his platoon had taken no particular notice of her why should she take any notice of him? All right, he had been different from the others in offering to help her and then spending a little time with her. But it wasn't as if she had said or done a single thing to give any hint of interest in him. Perhaps she had even spotted one of the others – Anderson, perhaps, he was a good-looking bastard – and been disappointed that it wasn't him instead of Johnny who had come to help with the washing up. True, she'd been a bit embarrassed and nervous about looking at him but that was simply girls, they were shy, it didn't mean anything. Maybe she really didn't want to look at him, all red in the face and wearing that stupid army uniform – and in his stockinged feet, for heavens' sake! No girl, however desperate, could fancy that. And here was another thing: a girl as pretty as Jane would be very likely to have a boyfriend already. Being a day girl she had plenty of opportunity to meet boys, and then working in a pub probably put her in the way of young men. Also it was known that girls liked boys older than themselves. Of course he couldn't tell how old she was but there couldn't be much in their ages. He was very far from being the older, good-looking, romantic type so what chance had he anyway? His heart sank. There was just one thing, though. At the end she had made that funny little comment to her mother about Johnny doing washing up at home. That didn't mean she fancied him – of course not, silly idea – but it did at least show that she had taken in something about him.

What to do next? This question kept on coming up. He had asked it of himself and of Angus as early as his first sighting of her at the dance. He had asked it afterwards and then after the encounter with the girls from her school. Now fate had done the job for him in throwing them together – that was a good sign, wasn't it? – but he certainly couldn't go on relying on that. He had taken matters into his own hands in going into the kitchen at the pub – he was proud of that – but though that had pushed him one stage further, to actually meeting her and talking to her, it didn't really get him off the runway. The question remained: what should he do next? Well this time he had an idea.

'My plan is this,' Johnny explained to Angus soon after the events of Field Day. 'You know I told you Jane's father stood us all that food and drink, he didn't charge a penny, well, I'm going to have a whip-round amongst the platoon, collect some money and then take it to him at the Rose and Crown. It won't be the full amount, of course, but it would be a gesture. With a bit of luck she'll be there, on a Saturday or Sunday.'

'In case you'd forgotten, pubs are out of bounds,' commented Angus rather drearily, Johnny thought. 'What about sending some flowers – women love flowers.'

'Do they? Why?'

'I don't know. They just do. There's lots of things like that about women.'

'Oh, are there? Well, should I send them to Mrs Baxter, then? That's a good idea. I couldn't send them direct to Jane, could I? – it would look too obvious.'

'Why not write first? Mr Baxter won't want money but he'll appreciate appreciation.'

'That's an idea. Jane would see the letter at any rate, and that would tell her I'm a good chap.'

Angus refrained from pointing out that girls didn't fall for boys because they were good chaps who helped with the washing up: Johnny would have to learn that himself.

'It's a start,' he said. Angus' interest was waning. He had listened to Johnny's account of the famous meeting at Bockington and endured his friend's excitement for some time but the generosity of his nature was being pushed so that when Johnny started discussing what kind of writing paper he should use for his letter Angus apologised and left.

In the end Johnny decided that he would write direct to Jane rather than to one of her parents. Why not? After all, he wasn't just being polite, was he? He had a romantic cause to pursue and if it looked a bit odd, well, so what?

'Dear Jane,' he began. That was the easy bit. Although Angus, in his correspondence, was well into 'My dearest Angela' he, Johnny, was at a quite different level. What hadn't been so easy was the choice of paper. Of course he had the Basildon Bond his parents provided him with so that he could write to them each week, as he did, but somehow it didn't have quite that special quality the occasion demanded so he decided to splash out and buy at the Tucker a small supply of the crested writing paper with the address of his house on it. It was expensive and he couldn't put it on the bill for fear of paternal questions but it looked great. Too great, perhaps. Maybe he shouldn't give an impression of being 'grand' – Worthington wasn't grand at all (Nick apart) but Jane, going to a state school, might think it was and be off-put. In that case, maybe he should just write on ordinary school exercise paper. It would be more sort of true to life and casual, as if writing was no big deal – she needn't think he was pathetically overdoing it or attaching too much importance to the communication, as if he regularly wrote that kind of letter. But then mightn't that look a bit too casual? In the end he temporised and wrote on exercise paper, calling it a first draft if he made mistakes and needed to redo it, at which point he could decide what kind of paper it would be best to use for the *real* thing. And then there was the equally difficult matter of what he would write *with*...

'Dear Jane, (I hope you don't mind if I call you that) I wanted to write and say how much my friends and I appreciated your hospitality the other day. It was really kind of your father to do so much for us and give us all that food and drink, not to mention help us win the battle and then drive us back to school. Will you please thank him for us.' (He made no mention of the awkward consequences of her father's kindness.) Now what? 'I really enjoyed drying up with you'? Oh, dry up! And then he had a brilliant idea. 'You may wonder why I am writing to you instead of direct to your father, well, the reason is I was wondering whether he might consider giving me a job at the pub. This is a bit of cheek, I know, but I did just think things must be busy at the week-ends and – as you know – I do know how to wash up!! I know I am not old enough to serve at the bar or anything but I know there are lots of jobs that need doing, like the ones you do and I don't mind getting my hands dirty! And I don't need paying a lot, in fact... ' – another brilliant idea – 'I would like to do it as sort of paying back for all that food and drink.' In truth he wouldn't mind crawling across the car park picking up cigarette stubs and broken glass with his bare hands if it would get him to the Rose and Crown but – hey, steady on! 'So I hope you don't mind me making this suggestion and I look forward to hearing from you. Yours... ' – well, here was a difficulty. 'Yours sincerely,' seemed too formal but by no means could he get any more friendly than that. 'Yours truly'? A tiny bit warmer but none too pushy: he'd settle for that. He added 'I hope you are well. Yours truly, Johnny Clarke. (JOHN CLARKE)'

Johnny was mighty pleased with this. Without launching into a confession or declaration or anything at all like that, he had been able to address her and what's more in such a way as to ensure that she would write back to him. And in her turn, she didn't have to be at all committal – it wasn't as if he was asking her out or saying, 'Will you be my pen friend?' (yeuch). But it might be the crucial next stage and move him into a position – working alongside her – on which he could build. It was also a bit of a test. She could think Who is this tiresome boy? – and write a short note to say there were no vacancies at the Rose and Crown at present. Yours sincerely. Or indeed not even reply at all! But then again she could say it was nice of him to write and she appreciated his help with the washing up and if he'd like to come on over then he would be welcome though she wasn't sure her father would be able to pay him. Would he like to come along one day anyway and see? Yours truly. 'P.S. I get back from school at about four o'clock each day if you are able to come along early one evening.' Then that would give him some idea of her attitude towards him.

In all this, though, it was curious, wasn't it? He didn't for a moment say to himself, 'I've only met her once and merely exchanged a few words with her: I wonder if I'll like her when I know her better.' It was simply: 'I love her and the more I see her the more I will love her.' For all the dithering he did over what to do when, where, how etc., there was absolutely not a moment's dither about his feeling for her. In his enthusiasm, however, he had skated over the issue of how he was going to get to Bockington and of the risks involved in being in the pub (even if working rather than drinking). No one at school had a job during term time and he'd be in dead trouble if caught. In fact it would certainly mean gating and that would be very bad news for the relationship!

Heading for the porter's lodge to buy a stamp and post the letter, Johnny thought, If it goes this evening she'll get it tomorrow morning but then she's got school so she'd be pushed to answer it and post it that day in time for me to get it the day after tomorrow, so it's the next day at the earliest. That meant three nights and two whole days before he could hear back from her. How was he going to live through the time? How could he possibly concentrate on a single other thing? However, the two days and the three nights did pass and that first possible morning dawned bright. At breakfast Johnny eagerly watched the post boy as he sauntered up and down the breakfast table distributing letters. There was nothing for him, though. He tried not to be disappointed, reasoning that she would need to talk to her father about his working there before replying: that morning was the first possible morning. But when there was nothing the next day or the next he began to get really worried.

The worst fears blew through his imagination: she simply wasn't going to bother replying to this rather cheeky and boring letter from a virtual stranger of no interest to her. His cheeks burned with shame as he imagined her saying to her real boyfriend, 'Oh, would you believe it, I had this pathetic letter from one of those Worthington boys. Do you know what he said... ?' The whole thing was dead. It would have been better never to have seen her. Now life would be completely pointless and empty. Then a new possibility occurred to him: his letter had got lost in the post. So perhaps he should write again: 'Dear Jane, I know this might sound a bit odd but I wrote to you several days ago and as I haven't heard back from you I just wondered whether the letter was never delivered or something... ' Alternatively, of course, *her* letter had got lost. In a way, that would be worse because in the absence of a reply to her reply she would be thinking, What on earth's happened about that boy who wrote for a job and I wrote back and he hasn't bothered to be in touch? Such possibilities tortured his mind until the day when once again fortune stepped in on his behalf.

He was just off to the porter's lodge in the dead of mid-afternoon to ask the porter – when no one else was there to hear him – whether there had been, to his knowledge, a lot of cases recently of mail gone missing, when what should he see but Mr Baxter's trusty old Dormobile parked nearby and Mr Baxter himself unloading boxes from the back. The dear vehicle with its old-fashioned lines and its dreary colouring of brown and yellow (not including the rust) sent a shiver through his heart with its associations of the wonderful day and the hour of bliss in the Rose and Crown kitchen.

'Wine deliveries,' he explained on Johnny's greeting him. He had not exactly recognised the boy but Johnny had explained that he was one of those to whom he had been so kind on their Field Day. Oh yes, Mr Baxter laughed at the memory. 'That was a triumph, wasn't it?'

Johnny gave him a hand with the boxes, desperately trying to think how to get to the essential point. 'How's your daughter?' ? 'I wonder if Jane's had a letter from me?' ? 'Are you by any chance looking for another pair of hands at the week-end?'?

'Well, thanks young man,' said Mr Baxter as they finished. 'By the way I wonder if you could do one small thing for me. I've got a letter here somewhere… ' – and he fished in various pockets of his old tweed jacket – ' needs delivering to one of your chums. It's from my daughter… ' – and here he looked up with something of a twinkle in his eye. 'Perhaps you could pass it on to the lucky recipient.'

Johnny's heart plummeted: the letter was for someone else! Bloody Anderson, probably, had got in before him. He hadn't sat around agonizing about what kind of bloody paper to write on – he probably hadn't bothered with writing at all, he'd upped and gone right back to the Rose and Crown and chatted her up and now here they were in the depths of an amorous correspondence. Curses, damn and bugger-blast!

'It's for – ' Mr Baxter flipped the letter – an ordinary correspondence-size envelope – right side up to read the direction. 'It's for… a Johnny Clarke – do you know him?'

Johnny Clarke? Oh yes, he knew him all right. Thank you, Mr Baxter. I'll take it.

Of course the letter was far too much of a treasure to be opened and read at once. Johnny put it away in the breastpocket of his jacket and sauntered away, ever so nonchalant, to be on his own. His study wasn't safe enough – someone might come in. The bogs were private enough but not quite the place for so lofty and wondrous an experience. He made for Gethsemane – there'd be no one there. As he walked, Johnny put his hand inside the jacket to feel the envelope almost as if to prove to himself that it was actually there. It felt quite thick. Then he drew it out, albeit in a public place but putting on a slight frown as if he were consulting his school calendar. All at once he realised that though he had thought of nothing else but her possible reply ever since he'd written to her he found now that he was completely unprepared for it. What was she going to say?

He must prepare himself for a negative response. Well, that was perfectly possible – he mustn't think that just because she had replied that reply was favourable. It could read, 'Dear Mr Clarke' (no, surely not); 'Dear Johnny, My father appreciated your letter of thanks. About working here, though, he says that unfortunately… ' Johnny's blood ran cold at the thought. Then, to cheer himself up, he ran the opposite scenario. 'My Dear Johnny, I was so thrilled to get your letter. It may sound surprising but I'd been hoping you'd write as I so enjoyed our chat in the kitchen even if we were only doing the washing up and I was hoping we might be able to meet again… ' Well, some hope.

Arrived at the secret garden, Johnny sat on the purloined bench and with a palpitating heart took out the blue envelope. On the front was written in a neat, rounded handwriting – why did only girls have handwriting like that? – : Johnny Clarke, Meyrick House, Worthington College, Worthington, Sussex. Johnny Clarke, eh? To think, her own hand, her own pen, had actually written his name! The letter was quite thick. Didn't that rule out the worst possibility – if she was going to say

'Sorry, no' that wasn't going to take more than one sheet of paper, was it?

Well, time to open it. Using the cardboard edge of his College calendar as a knife – he didn't want any ragged edges on his treasure – Johnny, holding his breath, carefully slit open the letter. It contained two sheets and ran as follows:

'Dear Johnny, Thank you very much for your letter which I got yesterday. Quite a surprise as I don't normally get any letters except at my birthday. My dad was very pleased that you had taken the trouble to write and thank him. He had such a good time with you that was reward enough for him I can tell you.' Johnny exhaled in relief: it was OK, it was OK!! 'About working at the pub he says the best thing is to come over one day and spend some time here and see how you get on. I told him that you were a very handy drier-upper (!)' (swoon, swoon) 'and I was sure that you could be a great help. To be honest, though, I'm not sure he can afford it. He said, 'If I pay him (meaning you, of course) then I'll have to pay you (meaning me!)!!' Anyway, why don't you do that? I realise it might be difficult for you to get here being at boarding school but please feel free to come when you can.'

Well, could it have been better? No, it bloody well couldn't!

There was more. 'Sorry I wasn't all that talkative when you came into the kitchen to help that day. I'm normally very talkative – my mum says I never stop! – but I was a bit taken aback, particularly as you were dressed like a soldier which I am not used to! Perhaps I should tell you a little about myself' – oh, God! – 'I am fifteen (nearly sixteen) and I go to school at the High School in Bishopstown where I am taking my O Levels this summer. I am doing English Language and English Literature, Maths, French, Latin and Science, so I am really trying to work hard. I play netball and the piano. I haven't got any brothers or sisters which has advantages and disadvantages! I read quite a lot. All I know about you at the moment is that you do the drying up at home! Are you doing O Levels? I think you might be a bit older than me so perhaps you are doing A

Levels. Where do you live? Is it a long way away? I would really like to hear a bit more about you when you come (if you want to come, that is) or by letter if you have the time to write, I expect you are very busy at school. Yours... ' – now here was the crunch – 'Yours with very good wishes, Jane (Baxter).'

The letter loose in his hand, Johnny leant back on the bench with a deep sigh – no, a groan – of satisfaction. This was it: they were on. There was no mistaking her sincere interest. To be sure, it was not a love letter – well, why should it be? – but there was more than enough there to give Johnny encouragement, not least in the superscription where the word 'very' had been added later, written in above the words 'with' and 'good' with a little chinaman's hat underneath. That showed she'd thought about it; it showed she'd wanted to make the farewell just a touch warmer. Ooh, lovely, lovely, lovely!

Little prep, if any, did Johnny get done that night, as he covered several sides of the Tucker's best house writing paper in his reply. Don't overdo it now, he thought, but he could barely contain himself in all he wanted to say. It was just really talking to her, that's what he wanted to be doing, it was not the imparting of information, and this was the nearest he could get to chatting to her – for the time being anyway. But that time being, he determined, would not be long.

✳ CHAPTER 11 ✳

A Game of
Scrabble

The School bicycle sheds were situated on a sunless slope of the College's periphery between the old fives courts and the estate offices (out of bounds). They were actually a single building but pluralised in common parlance and occasionally referred to as Golgotha for reasons that may become apparent. It had been built at a time when the possession of a bicycle was almost general: serried ranks of them, organised by houses and innocent of locks, filled the racks, their front wheels aloft in their metal runners like cattle at a feeding trough. This method of transport had, however, declined in popularity and 'the sheds' now bore an air of neglect. It was more than half empty. There was an increasing amount of unlawful 'borrowing' and consequent lack of mechanical care devoted to the machines. More and more of them were in need of repair, many beyond it. Here was one without a front wheel, there one saddleless; here a mere frame and there one with a back wheel so bent as to be useless. Flat tyres were endemic. Everywhere, the broken and the cannibalised lay like the aftermath of some ghastly velocipedal holocaust.

The decline in the sheds' proper function brought a growth in the improper. It was here that the occasional act of orchestrated persecution might be carried out as society saw fit and away from adult eyes, and it was here that a personal dispute might be settled, an encounter rendered semi-official by the presence and adjudication of a school prefect, to the gratification of a sizeable crowd. Less dramatically, it had become the haunt of smokers, as the condition of the floors testified, fag ends featuring prominently amongst the crisp packets and sweet wrappers which it was no one's job to sweep up. Only in one corner did the old standards prevail. Here the school Cycle Club zealously maintained a wreck-free area, models of the newest type with shiny paint and chrome, slim leather saddles and derailleur gears, nestled together for companionship, each secured with a prominent lock. And it was to this area that Johnny came one Saturday after cricket to do a recce in search of a bike that might serve his purposes. (To be the owner of a bicycle when past the Fifth Form was as good as to declare oneself a social failure, so naturally he had ceased, to his parents' incomprehension, bringing his to school.) Since anyone owning a bike had to paint his name clearly on the machine itself, it was possible for Johnny to see who owned what and to whom he must therefore be nice if he was to borrow one, for that was his intention.

The talk of going to the Rose and Crown and helping out there had come down, for practical and disciplinary reasons, to Sunday lunch. 'Going on a bike ride' was a perfectly legitimate leisure activity and if he could get away promptly after morning chapel Johnny could reach Bockington well before midday and would not need to return till after tea for Evensong. His survey of the Cycle Club's armoury identified a bike belonging to Erf – aka Sergeant Frost – as the most suitable. It was, to be sure, rather a smart affair with narrow tyres and trim little mudguards not to mention the complicated gears now *de rigueur* amongst serious cyclists and Erf might well be reluctant to lend it for he was not only a leading light in the Club but also the sort of person whose concern for his own possessions ruled out lending them for fear of loss or damage. However, Erf was susceptible to flattery and blandishment and Johnny decided on an approach to his fellow officer.

Success attended his efforts and the next morning after Eucharist he lost no time in getting to the bike sheds, whither Erf had, however, insisted on accompanying him in order to 'show him the ropes' of his proud machine. How difficult was it to ride a bicycle? thought Johnny, as Erf wittered on about the gear changes, but he was soon on the road and pedalling like hell northwards. Past the tiny church of St Basil in a dell, over dikes and up hills, he raced, the derailleur gear system – in spite of some gruesome scrunching – proving useful on the slopes. It was a lovely day, the sun shining and the wind whistling through his hair as he rose in the pedals to relish it on the downhill. What would it be like, he wondered, when he got there? Would she be very busy with pub work and hardly able to pay him any attention, or would they even get any time to themselves, during afternoon closing perhaps? And if they did, where would they go and what would they do? They had now exchanged two letters each and although there had been no upgrading of the language – no promotion of 'Dear Jane' to 'My Dear Jane', as might be hoped for in the future, and no mention at all of feelings – they had exchanged hundreds of words and now knew quite a lot about each other.

It turned out to be a busy morning at the Rose and Crown and the garden tables were soon full of customers to whom Johnny and Jane ministered busily while Mr and Mrs Baxter worked flat-out in bar and kitchen respectively. Johnny could not imagine doing anything more enjoyable, he and Jane, continuously passing each other in the car park, seeing each other at the tables, meeting briefly in the kitchen. There was no call for conversation as such, no occasion for self-consciousness, just looks and smiles exchanged, a few words – 'Which table is this?', 'Can you take those?' Gradually, however, the bustle died down and the customers drifted away into the summer Sunday afternoon.

'I don't need paying, Mr Baxter,' said Johnny triumphantly as the door closed on the final drinker. 'Look at the tips!' and he displayed a double handful of coins.

'And I've got as much,' put in Jane. 'Best this season!'

'I'm not surprised,' said Mr Baxter, 'you did a wonderful job out there, you two. It's been a terrific morning. Now let's get some lunch ourselves.'

By the time their own lunch was over the sunny day had soured and greyed over and a slight drizzle had started. So much for the nice walk Johnny had hoped for. There was still a couple of hours before he need set off back to school and he had hoped for some time alone with Jane on the Downs.

'I'll deal with these,' said Mrs Baxter, indicating the plates at the sink. 'You two have done your bit for today.'

So there they were, 'you two'. Johnny liked the sound of that: it was as if Mrs Baxter were pairing them off approvingly. No work to distract them from each other, nothing to prevent them from just having time together. An acute self-consciousness overcame them both: what were they to do? The stand-by 'Let's go for a walk' was ruled out by the weather and the recourse of childhood – 'What would you like to play?' – they were too old for.

'And I'll be off for my snooze,' said Mr Baxter.

Mrs Baxter said helpfully, 'Why don't you two go to the sitting-room?'

This turned out to be a smallish room upstairs in the old house, the major, downstairs rooms being of course given over to the bars. There they sat facing each other across a cold fireplace.

'Almost cold enough to have a fire,' commented Jane, staring hard into the empty grate.

'Bit different from the last time I came here.'

'Yes,' she laughed, picking unconsciously at the little hairy bits on the arm of the sofa. 'Do you have a gramophone?'

'No, I don't. Some of my friends do. Have you got one?'

'No, I haven't.'

'But you play the piano, don't you? So I expect you've got one here at home.' Johnny looked around the small room, more to give his eyes a break from the strain of catching her eye or avoiding doing so than in search of such an instrument that, however modestly upright, it would have been impossible not to notice on entry into so limited a space.

'It's downstairs,' she replied, 'in the bar. I practise when we're closed.'

'Oh. Are you very good at it?'

'I've just done my Grade Three.'

'Is that very advanced?'

She laughed. 'No, not at all. I'm not very good really. Are you musical?'

'I can sing,' Johnny replied, then added hastily lest he might at some future time be taken up on this or – worse – lest it should be taken as a boast, 'What I mean is, I can sing hymns and so on all right – but I can't read music.' And then he thought of the film that he and the company had been to see on the night of the fire engine. 'And there's a tune I like in a film I've just seen. Of course I can't exactly remember the tune off the top of my head,' he added quickly.

'The last film I saw was *Summer Sun*.'

'That's the one! That's the film I mean.'

'Oh yes, that had a lovely catchy tune, didn't it?

'Yes, I've been humming it all week.'

'And did you like the film itself?' she asked.

'Oh I did, I really did. It was so… ' But how could he go on? He couldn't really say, 'I loved that bit when they were walking along the beach at sunset in bare feet and then they started running, weaving in and out of each other's paths across the sand.'

'It was very sad in the end, wasn't it?' said Jane. 'I cried.' She looked a little anxiously at him as if to determine his reaction to this confession.

'Well, I nearly did,' said Johnny and they both laughed.

There was a slightly awkward pause during which neither looked at the other. Johnny was tempted to glance at his watch just to see how the time was going. He really mustn't be late for roll-call, he couldn't afford any more trouble after the Field Day business. In a sense he was desperate to get away – to escape the pressure of this situation that he'd never been in before and which he didn't think he was managing at all well. And if he did he could take away with him a fresh and wonderful image of her sitting on the sofa and them chatting happily about things. On the other hand, if he did get away, where would he most want to be? – here, with her, of course. Besides, what about their next meeting?

'Tell me about your school,' Jane then said, tucking her legs up on the sofa and resettling there as if to make herself comfortable for a good long spell as audience.

'Well, what do you want to know?'

'Everything!' she laughed awkwardly.

'You know what school's like,' he said. Really, what was there to say? School was school. You worked, played games, mucked about and so on.

'I've never been at a boarding school, you see,' she said, adding, 'though I have read some stories set in a girls' boarding school.'

Johnny, who had always been at boarding school, didn't know what to tell her. 'Well, you get a bit fed up with it sometimes, you feel a bit locked in – that's why it's fun to go outside occasionally. My friends and I… ' –

'Yes, tell me about your friends,' she put in eagerly.

'Well, my best friend's Angus. He was at the dance, you know, where you were helping with the drinks. Not that you'd have known which one he was. Anyway we see a lot of each other and tell each other about things. He's got a girlfriend, called Angela. He met her at the dance. I helped him write a letter to her afterwards – well, I wrote the letter really, he's not a great writer – not that I am either, of course, it's just that when it's not you it's maybe easier to… say things.'

Jane's features suddenly became somewhat downcast. Oh dear, he'd said the wrong thing. 'Don't you think?' he added desperately.

'I don't know,' said Jane, leadenly. 'I've never written that sort of letter... and you obviously have.' There seemed a tone of reproach in her voice.

'Oh no,' said Johnny quickly. 'Not on my own account, not for myself.'

'Then how can you write it for someone else if you don't... if you haven't got experience of that sort of... relationship?'

'Well, you imagine, don't you? I mean you don't have to 'have experience' to say things like, 'I thought your dress looked great,' or, 'It would be super to see you sometime,' or, 'I loved your letter' – you know. That kind of thing.'

Oh dear, this wasn't helping. Jane seemed to have slumped. He'd said the wrong thing and then gone on to say something even wronger. How sad she looked! Suddenly his heart went out to her. 'Actually I didn't enjoy the dance very much. I didn't... meet anyone like Angus met Angela. Do you remember seeing me at the dance?' he asked carefully.

'I do,' she said simply.

Oh, God, he'd hit the buffers here. Diversion, quick – diversion!

'I say, what's *Scrabble?*' His eye had lit on a box on the table with that word printed on it.

'It's a word game,' Jane answered, matter-of-factly.

'Oh? Is it good?'

'Quite good.' No spark yet.

'Shall we play?' Anything to escape the pressure of this situation he seemed to have got into.

'If you like.'

'Where's the best place to play?'

'On the floor probably.' Jane rose unhurriedly to pick up the box and lay the contents on the carpet. Johnny was glad to get up and move a bit. They settled down, facing each other, he leaning chin on hand, she, her skirt deftly tucked beneath her, more upright. 'Well what you do is... ' she began without enthusiasm, and explained the game.

'You score,' he said, 'my Maths is hopeless.'

After a few turns Johnny said, 'Ooh, I've got a good one – if I can get it on a triple, that is. Are you allowed proper names, by the way?'

'No.'

'Oh! I say, let's play that you get bonus points if you do a word that's sort of relevant. I mean like 'pub' or 'sandwich' or –

'– sausage!' Wow, that was almost a smile.

'Or two-pints-of-shandy-and-a-double-whisky-please.' She was smiling! 'Or, this – ' and here Johnny laid out 'JANE'. 'It's not on a triple but it is on a double.'

'And if you had a T,' said Jane, 'you could do 'Janet', and score even more.'

'Oh no, I couldn't,' Johnny replied, 'because there's no one called Janet hereabouts and anyway I am completely and totally satisfied with JANE.'

'It may sound silly,' she said, 'but when I was smaller I longed to be called Janet. I thought Jane was so plain and dull and Janet sounded much more superior.'

'That's because of those Janet and John books. Hey, that's us – Janet and John. No, I mean Jane and Johnny – that's best.'

At last Jane seemed to have cheered up a bit, to Johnny's relief, as if playing the game had lightened her heart somehow. He hadn't time to think about it now but somebody had said that girls were different, they didn't always react to things as boys did and didn't always want the same things. Flowers, for instance, as Angus had suggested sending to Mrs Baxter; he said women liked flowers. OK, it would be odd not to like flowers, a bit anyway, but why should someone be touched if you gave them flowers? All that happened was that they went into a vase, looked pretty for a while and then died. What was so touching about that? Mystery. Obviously he had a lot to learn. Anyway, he was really enjoying himself, making clever words, and when she made a slip in the scoring he said she was cheating because she couldn't make points any other way and then she put down LONER and he said if she had a V she could make that LOVER and she had and scored much more which he said should be added to his score and she said nonsense but then he put a P on the front of LOVER which he argued should be a bonus because plovers were a common feature on the Downs and she said that was pushing it. And he agreed.

As they played, their positions on the floor were constantly changing. After a while they were both outstretched, supported on an arm and a hand splayed on the floor. Johnny noticed that their hands were not all that far apart so when it was his turn he took the opportunity to inch his hand just a little closer to hers. Just a little. He didn't want her to think he was doing it on purpose, it had to appear completely natural and unpremeditated. But then, as the game wore on, he began to worry that she might move away her hand which up till then – since he had embarked on this approach, anyway – had not moved at all, so the next time he covered more ground, shifting his whole position as a cover-up, until he realised that if he moved it any further he would be touching her hand. He was finding it hard to concentrate on the game now, making one or two rather feeble scores, but coincidentally she seemed to have lost her spark for it as well so perhaps it didn't show. Now for it. He had made it. Or had he? That is, he'd made the move all right but was he touching? He didn't now dare look as she might see him looking and think he'd done it on purpose. Surely his hand had come to a stop against something but he couldn't feel anything. That's because his finger was completely still, if he moved it a bit he would -

'Cup of tea, anyone?' Mrs Baxter had opened the door.

'Oh, thank you,' said Johnny slowly as if coming out of a sleep. 'Crikey, is that the time? I'd better be on my way.' He scrambled to his feet. Jane remained on the floor, silent, her hand just where he had left it.

❊ CHAPTER 12 ❊

A Trip to
Clouds

Johnny's departure from the Rose and Crown was somewhat hurried. He said his thank-yous politely enough but he left too quickly to dwell on his farewell to Jane or to say anything about any future meeting. Coward. Of course he wanted one but he needed time to think when and where. The Rose and Crown was good – well away from school – but then her parents were very much there which was a bit cramping, friendly to him though they were. Perhaps they should meet in Bishopstown.

Anyway, that had gone all right, hadn't it? he reflected, pedalling hard – and now against the wind – back to school. Certainly there was some awkwardness on both their parts to begin with, particularly when they were just talking in the sitting-room. Just talking in anyone's sitting-room was not Johnny's idea of a good time – he preferred to be doing things – so maybe that was why he had gone off the rails somehow in his talk about Angus and writing his letter to Angela for him. That had gone down really badly and he'd only succeeded in making it worse.

But *Scrabble* had saved the day. Somehow that had lightened things up a bit and she seemed to enjoy herself. And then there were the hands. Now when it came to submitting to Angus' enquiries – not to say inquisition – the following morning in

Latin, it was not going to be any good saying, 'We touched fingers – or I think we did, I couldn't exactly tell.' Touching fingers in Angus' lexicon of amorous acts was plainly illiterate and would deservedly bring down on him Angus' scorn. No, it wasn't much, that was true, although it was an advance on the previous position even if – and this was crucial – he could not positively say that there had been any reaction on her part. Had she welcomed his approaching hand? Had there been any movement against his? He couldn't honestly say there had been. And yet how could he convey to Angus the sudden intimacy in the atmosphere (what was 'atmosphere' to Angus?), the intense feeling of excitement as he inched closer?

He must get those famous gears into action – crunch, scrunch – go on, you bastard, down, down… crikey, that didn't sound quite right… oh, God! the gears were stuck, not broken, he could still pedal, thank goodness, but stuck in high gear. That was fine for the flat and the downhill but uphill it would be hopeless. He would have to get off and walk – or run, rather – if there was any hope of catching roll-call. Oh bugger!

Soon, hard though he pedalled, fast though he ran, he could see he wasn't going to make it. Well, that wasn't a total disaster. Of course he would be missed but he could get round the prefect concerned and as long as he actually made it to chapel he could get away with it. The problem with Erf's bike and possible repercussions there, financial or otherwise, were minor at the moment and could wait. He must make it to chapel. He pictured the Horse in his pew scanning the house rows, noticing his absence, checking with him later. 'Not in chapel, Clarke?' 'No, sir' 'Where were you?' 'Bicycle broke down, sir.' After that it would depend. With a bit of luck – no, with a lot of luck – he might get away with it but he sort of had the feeling that the Horse was not all that happy with him at the moment. Johnny had come into the school as a sound sort of chap and had now fallen in with some dubious company – smokers, at the very least, not to mention somewhat bolshy – gone off the rails on Field Day and now here he was on a bicycle expedition to who knew where or why. That would be gating, and the Horse would have him reporting in twice daily. Bugger. Pedal, man, pedal.

But to no avail. As he sweated up the College drive he could hear the chapel bell ringing, see the trail of boys heading for the west door, a trail already thinning as the hour approached. There was no lee-way with these prefects: 6.29 and 59 seconds was fine – maybe even 6.30 at a pinch – but 6.30 and one second – not a chance. Dumping the bike behind a buttress of the nave, Johnny, scrambling his suit jacket back on, tore up the path to the main entrance – just in time to see the scarlet hood of the choirmaster following his boys in procession up the nave and the two waistcoated prefects close the heavy west doors in his face.

A lesson with Dr Cust on Monday morning provided a good opportunity for Johnny to go over things with Angus as they sat at the back at a double desk with the Livy crib out of sight between them. Dr Cust was a temporary appointment relieving the Wolf who had been standing in recently for an absent master. This Dr Cust was a complete walkover. How the Wolf – fairly canny in such matters – had allowed himself to engage the services of such an obvious incompetent even on a temporary basis it was hard to say, for Dr Cust was old, not in the sense that every adult was old, but visibly aged, almost decrepit, being small and stooped, grey-haired and slow of movement. The classroom to which he had been assigned was one of the grander chambers giving off the Library and boasted not only a dais for the master's desk but a somewhat grandiose – almost throne-like – chair. Dr Cust, perched there, was too small to extend his little feet fully to the ground so that they hung loosely in midair like a child's. In such an undignified position he had no chance of commanding respect. Added to this, he was a bit deaf, a defect exploited by the boys who deliberately spoke to him in low tones. His lessons, therefore, passed in an amiable atmosphere of chat and not a little coming and going of an unjustified nature. 'Matron wanted to see me at ten o'clock, sir.' 'Why?' 'I'm not sure, sir. I think it's to do with the polio injections.' ' Oh, very well.' The poor man's lack of grip on his class enabled another member of the form, Greg Glass, to bring his beloved mouth organ into the lesson, executing deft little riffs when Doctor Cust wasn't looking and whipping it up his sleeve when he was.

'So now you've gone and got yourself gated, you idiot,' was Angus' comment.

'Not my fault. It's not fair, is it – Nick spends an evening in a nightclub in Mayfair and gets away with it while I'm gated for being one minute late for chapel!'

'So where does that leave you with Jane?'

'Bloody nowhere.'

'Back to the Basildon Bond, eh?'

'Looks like it.'

'Bad luck. Of course I could go and see her for you if you like,' his friend volunteered.

Johnny hesitated. Some human contact, even if vicarious, would be better than nothing but then it would be horribly unsatisfying. Of course he trusted his friend completely – it wasn't that he would be jealous or anything – but he would be envious of his seeing her and that would make his imprisonment worse.

'Is that music, I hear?' Dr Cust then queried, lifting his head like some bemused bovine.

'I believe it is, sir. Saunders' study, I expect. I'll go and tell him to shut up, shall I, sir? Won't be a minute.' Exit volunteer in full knowledge that the music emanated from Greg's mouth organ.

'How long's the gating?' Angus asked, resuming their private conversation.

'Till half-term.'

'No Isle of Wight then.'

'I suppose not – hadn't thought of that.' Not that the cricket match on the island was now quite the excitement it would have been without Jane to think of.

'Clarke next, please,' then came the quavering voice from the dais just above the gentle hubbub in which they were all immersed.

'Sir?'

'Continue the construe, please.'

'Yes, sir.' To Angus: Where the hell are we? Angus to Johnny: No idea. 'I think I may have slightly lost the place, sir.'

'Not been following, Clarke?'

'I wouldn't say that exactly, sir. I was kind of wondering about the construction in the second sentence, sir, and then kind of lost it.'

'I see. Arkwright, 'kind of' show Clarke where we are.'

The aforementioned boy, one of the few actually following the official proceedings with half an ear, obliged. Oh, curses – this passage was way beyond the point to which he had prepared.

'You did get this far, I take it, Clarke?' queried the little man, his white fingers bunched and gesturing feebly, as Johnny failed to utter.

'Oh, Gosh, yes sir!' Luckily by this time Angus had got an accurate bearing on their position in the crib so that Johnny was able to put into practice the ignoble art of construing from a ready-made text while giving the impression that he was doing so from memory, with suitable pauses, and the odd stumble and going back, the occasional minor error.

'Not bad, Clarke. Beta-minus.'

'Oh, sir!'

'Well, beta then.'

'Thank you, sir.'

So letters it was. First a thank-you – with suitable note to parents – for the visit on Sunday and then a fairly detailed account of the hectic ride back to school and its sad consequences for their meeting again soon. 'I should have left earlier but I was so enjoying that game we were playing that I forgot how late it was.' This was as near as he could get to referring to that wonderful moment when he actually made contact (or was fairly sure he had made contact) with her hand on the floor. After that there was not a lot to say. But he wrote and posted promptly and sat back impatiently waiting for her reply.

Which soon came. It was a great deal longer than his. This was partly owing to the fact that girls' handwriting was almost always bigger than boys' and that they seemed to need to take more words to say the same amount, writing as if they were talking. 'It's such a pity about your gating, it must be so boring stuck in school all the time as you said even if it is a chance to get some work done and of course I'm sorry you won't be able to come out to the Rose and Crown again soon as you were a great help that Mum and Dad really appreciated – I did too as it meant I didn't have to do everything myself which would have been hard work with so many people. Yes,' she went on, 'I enjoyed the game of *Scrabble* too, even if you did accuse me of cheating (not really!!). We usually play it at the table but it was rather fun playing on the floor wasn't it' – ooh, this was getting warm – 'so much more relaxed. I hope we can play again some time.' But that was it. The rest of the letter was about school, a netball match and revision and how before O Levels they were allowed a day off per week for home revision – an impossibly wonderful idea to Johnny's mind. 'I know you say that you haven't got much to write about because it's only school but honestly I am interested in that as your school is so different from mine. Or are you having to spend a lot of time writing Angus's love letters for him?!?!' – oh, dear, that again – ' I can tell that you would be very good at it even if... ' – and the 'even if' was crossed out, the sentence brought instead to a full stop. 'even if' what? She ended, 'With warm good wishes.' Well, that was something, that was one up from 'with very good wishes'; 'warm' was definitely promising. He must follow that up.

Not long afterwards Johnny was in his study with the crested house writing paper. He was about to start, as customary, 'Dear Jane', but sat back, paused a moment, and then wrote 'My Dear Jane'. Things were moving on, after all.

The Horse was of a gentle and forgiving nature whose wrath was swift to pass so that when it came to deciding on the team for the Isle of Wight match and Johnny's name was put forward by the Hawk, the master-in-charge of the trip, the kind housemaster let it go through. It was after all a school event, not a jolly or a private expedition. Day trips away from the College, with the exception of the annual CCF Field Day, were unknown, but there was another element to this visit to Mr Kendal's school, which was called Clouds, that raised its interest and status still further, and that was that it involved an overnight stay. The Isle of Wight was not far but what with train and boat and cricket it was going to be a bit of a rush, the authorities judged, so why not get the team over the evening before, enjoy some sort of social with the boys and girls – yes, the school was co-educational (another factor in the trip's favour) – before a full day's cricket the next day with a return in good time that evening? Johnny made the most of this event in his letter to Jane, promising a full account of it afterwards. She expressed due interest in reply, stating that she had been to the island on several occasions because she had an aunt there. She envied him, she said, as she was stuck at home with her endless revision. She seemed to Johnny to be doing a lot of that; he couldn't remember anything so intense when he did his O Levels the previous summer but then perhaps that was why he had failed his Maths, which of course was coming up again to haunt him. Girls seemed to work harder than boys. The good thing was that just as he had begun his last letter with 'My Dear Jane' she had opened hers with 'My Dear Johnny', concluding it, as previously, 'With warm good wishes', an expression he had borrowed for his. They were as close as they could be to really saying something, to really expressing some feeling. Johnny was tempted to make his first real launch on paper where he was more confident and a lot safer but was determined not to go any further until he had seen her again. 'Actions first, words afterwards': that was Angus's advice and though it ran contrary to Johnny's nature he respected his friend's superior expertise and bowed to it. He knew what his feelings were but he didn't know about hers even if he sometimes allowed himself to hope: 'My Dear Johnny' and 'With warm good wishes' was not necessarily anything more than friendly.

There was a lot of hilarity amongst the group gathered in the outer quad that Friday afternoon, overnight bags in one hand, cricket bags in the other; blazers were the order of the day.

'Hey, do you reckon the Hawk's wife is coming as well?'

'Could be. Let's hope she wears that dress she was wearing for Litsoc.'

'I'll say!'

These hopes rose to warm expectation at the sight of her alongside her husband but were dashed as she remained behind when the group boarded the ancient coach that was to take them to the railway station for their onward journey to Portsmouth and so across the Solent by ferry. This disappointment was soon set aside, however, as they speculated about the prospects for the trip, not indeed of the cricket which was routine, but of the 'social' that they were to be entertained to that evening.

'Is 'a social' what you might call a dance, sir?' someone enquired of the Hawk.

'Not exactly,' came the reply. 'It's less formal than that, I believe.'

There was relief at that news.

'I suppose that, being co-ed, a dance isn't quite the same as with us, is it?'

'No, it seems they have what they call a 'social' for the senior boys and girls every fortnight or so.'

'What do they do if they don't dance?'

'Well… ' – the Hawk was fumbling a bit as his information

was thin and his experience nil but he did not want to appear ignorant – 'I believe they sit about and chat.'

'Is there any drink?'

'Possibly. And there's probably some music – records – which they dance to.'

'Hey, maybe it's rock-and-roll stuff.' And a group of the boys instantly went into the 'One o'clock, two o'clock, three o'clock rock' routine, Greg Glass strumming loudly on the guitar that he had, in addition to the mouth organ he was never without, brought with him. 'You can do a tune or two, Greg, give them one of your songs – you know, *On the Rainy Side of the Street.*

'Yeah, or *On.*' At which all broke into the tune that had become the theme tune of the group that Greg led, The Gees.

'All right, everyone,' the Hawk cautioned as this inharmonious riot quieted a little. 'Remember you're representing Worthington.'

To Johnny, who had been on no boat bigger than the Derwentwater pleasure steamer, the ferry was impressive and exciting and all the boys ran along the decks and up and down the stairs a good deal like little kids, buying foodstuffs and smoking where the Hawk, who sat decorously at a café seat puffing on his pipe, wouldn't see them, enjoying the sun and the wind and the coming and going of large ships in the channel. This beat Friday afternoon lessons!

The school, Clouds, was a ragged cluster of sandstone buildings perched more or less on the cliffs overlooking the Solent and back towards the south coast. Johnny's sense of excitement was given a further boost on arrival, for the first person he saw was a boy from his prep school.

'Tom, hi!'

Tom Bennett had not been the star of The Dell and had only made it to public school at all by his parents' choice of this somewhat alternative establishment, a progressive school, with its emphasis on the arts and crafts rather than games and academic success. Their prep school headmaster, Mr Victor, had dubbed him 'Nebbett' on account of his inveterate habit of transposing the letters of words, often the d's and the b's. This habit Mr Victor found incomprehensible, incorrigible and therefore unforgivable. Tom's forte was electrics, for which there had been little scope at The Dell. Here and now, however, was another matter, as he quickly demonstrated.

'Come and see the place for tonight's social,' he said, and led Johnny to a curious building that seemed like a converted chapel with a high vaulted ceiling and tall thin windows. 'This is the theatre,' he said. The stage was no more than a sizeable platform but it did boast an impressive lighting rig, with numerous rails and big black lanterns suspended; there were also footlights, with coloured gels. Much of this had an extemporised look which Johnny attributed to the skill and enthusiasm of his old friend but it was undoubtedly well in advance of anything at Worthington.

'This is my special,' said Tom, pointing up to a sort of wheel, perhaps a round of cardboard or something, with regular circular holes in, that was fixed in front of one of the lights. 'Wheel goes round,' Tom explained, 'light comes through holes and then gets blocked so you get a kind of come-and-go effect. My new invention – unveiled tonight,' he said with undissimulated pride.

Tom had certainly come on since those poor old days when he hadn't known a declension from a conjugation or how to hold a cricket bat, but now here he was, his own man, with surprisingly long hair and, in this theatre anyway, his own boss.

CHAPTER 13

Complications on
the Cliffs

To the astonishment of all the Worthington boys, they were allowed to smoke. A certain corner – the coffee bar corner, its name El Cappucino emblazoned in bold colours across the counter – was the permitted area of the theatre where the senior boys and girls of the school could light up whenever they wanted. They were not, however, allowed to smoke in other parts of the school, they explained, as this would set a bad example to the younger children. Johnny was not at all sure how he would like this. On the one hand it was extraordinarily liberal of the authorities to permit this practice; on the other hand there was something about nipping out to some favoured nook in the school grounds for a crafty gasper as a quietly defiant expression of independence. Perhaps the boys and girls at this school didn't need to be defiant. They certainly seemed quite relaxed about things, dressing as they liked and calling the staff – even the Headmaster – by their Christian names. Such a practice was inconceivable to Johnny: 'Here's my prep, Derek,' he could not imagine saying to the Burk. Otherwise they seemed just like anyone else and the Worthington boys, though still in school uniforms as they possessed no other clothes apart from cricket gear, mixed well with them. The host boys were pleasant without being actively hospitable and the girls took a slightly livelier interest: boy company they might routinely have but it was limited company and some new blood, if only transient, might be welcome. So Angus had argued in anticipation, even if there were one or two couples amongst them, including a boy and girl who clearly went around together all the time, even holding hands in public.

After the Headmaster, Mr Kendal, had given the Worthington boys a friendly welcome to Clouds, they had been escorted to the cafeteria (as they called it) where, instead of sitting down at tables and being waited on by fellow pupils, there was a queuing system. You picked up a tray on entry and passed along a line of food containers, taking what you wanted, collecting cutlery at the end of the line and then carrying your food-laden tray (meat and pudding at the same time) to the table and seat of your choice. It was all rather casual and seemed to work perfectly well.

'Far cry from meals at The Dell, eh, Tom?' said Johnny smiling.

'Compulsory semolina.'

'Staff crusts at Sunday breakfast.'

'This is much better, don't you think?'

'Much better.' Johnny cast his eye around the room, boys and girls coming and going. 'Hey, Tom, you got a girlfriend?'

'Nah, don't bother here – got other things to do. It can get in the way. I'm friendly with lots of girls but I don't have a girlfriend. You have one? – at home, I mean, obviously you couldn't have one at school.'

'Well, funny you should say that because as a matter of fact I... ' – but there Johnny was unable to go on because he couldn't honestly refer to Jane as a girlfriend. Sure, she was a girl and a friend but not a girlfriend. Perhaps that was all it was going to be, after all. 'I've never been just friends with a girl,' he said. 'Is it easy?'

Tom laughed. 'Just as easy as being friends with a boy. Easier sometimes. Girls aren't so competitive, they're more sympathetic if you're feeling down, that sort of thing. They like having boys as friends. They don't want to have nothing but boyfriends, if you see what I mean.' Johnny mulled over this novel concept. The slightly depressing thought that perhaps he and Jane were just friends and destined to stay that way, was beginning to entrench itself, unwelcome as it was, in his mind. 'All the same,' Tom added with a twinkle, 'that doesn't mean there won't be any girls taking an interest in you lot tonight.'

'Sounds promising,' said Angus, overhearing this.

'Remember Angela,' said Johnny piously.

'Yes,' Tom wound up, 'things can get quite lively at a social.'

Certainly the smoking arrangement was a good start and El Cappucino did really go some way to creating an atmosphere slightly different from normal school for it was not only possible to make coffee there but for the occasion some sort of fruit cup had been provided that seemed to Johnny to have a slight alcoholic content. Hey, this was a party!

The room had been blacked out against the long light summer evening and that created additional atmosphere. The lighting generally was very dim except on the stage where the gramophone was set up and where the school's band would play later. For the time being it was just drinking coffee and the fruit cup and smoking and chatting and wandering around and eyeing up the company. Some of the girls had changed into proper evening clothes – well, perhaps 'proper' was not quite the word, for many of the garments worn, though obviously party clothes, were distinctly informal. One girl had on a multi-coloured thing that came right down to the floor and seemed to be made of some rough sort of silk rather than the tulle or chiffon that Johnny was accustomed to as girls' party dress material. Another girl had divided her very long hair into several plaits ornamented with silver ribbon. One of the boys wore a black felt cowboy hat, another had teddy-boy creepers on and a black lace tie. Another girl was in mauve trousers.

'Makes us look a bit boring,' Johnny remarked to the girl sitting next to him. He had just lit her cigarette in a manly fashion.

'Oh no, you look great. I think your white shirts are really nice. A white shirt makes a man look so handsome.'

'Really?' Johnny was surprised. A white shirt was uniform; it was what you wore every day. How could it make you 'handsome'?

'Even a dirty one?' he queried, conscious that with shirt-change day on Wednesday the one he was wearing was not in its prime.

'Looks very clean in this light,' she laughed. 'What sort of music do you like? My name's Eva by the way.'

And so they got chatting.

Then the records came on. Tom had rigged up a superb sound system, with huge speakers, one in each corner of the room so that you got the music coming at you from all directions. Things warmed up a bit with people dancing in fairly random couples, in one or two cases girls together but nobody seemed to make much of it. Johnny danced with several girls, one of whom actually asked him to dance which had never happened to him before and which he rather liked: why should it always be the boys who had to take the first step? After a while there was a break before the band was announced. This was a group of four boys dressed in identical black shirts; one the singer, one the drummer, one on sax and one on electric guitar. They began to play some numbers that were known to the audience as the product of a professional group of black American singers. The present rendition did not shine by comparison and though there was polite applause at the end of this rather plodding performance it was probably more in recognition of Tom's new lighting effect with the rotating wheel which had prompted some cheers and wolf-whistles when it first came on than the prowess of the group.

'You have a go, Greg,' urged one of the visitors and Greg, who really needed some encouragement in the absence of the other members of the Gees by whom he was normally supported, stepped up to the stage with his guitar, to the partisan cheers of the Worthingtonians and the applause of the home team who looked on in polite expectancy. Greg's first effort was, like the previous song, a version of a well known rather soulful number with something of a story to it. He said, in introduction, it was a 'ballad'. The three top buttons of his shirt were opened to reveal a substantial gold crucifix beneath – he had slicked his hair and shoved his trousers as far down over his hips as possible in imitation of the song's original singer. He was listened to respectfully; there was a heartfelt warmth in his voice but it was not a particularly good one at that register. When the generous but far from overwhelming applause had died away he announced, 'Now I'm going to sing a song of my own; it's called *On*.'

A rather different note was now struck as Greg bent earnestly over his instrument and then lifted his head to belt out the opening bars. The Worthingtonians, knowing the song already, began to join in the refrain: 'On we go... we're moving on... we're on our way.' This was hardly difficult for others to pick up and soon everyone was belting it out. Then it developed into a sort of dance, not a specific step but a kind of swaying and hand-waving-cum-clapping that was initiated by a rather striking blonde girl, for not only was the tune catchy but it was rhythmic as well and there was something about the words of the song too that Greg reeled off with a clarity and emphasis that was quite novel. The volume increased. The home band behind the visiting singer began tentatively at first and then with more brio to participate on their instruments, the vocalist coming up alongside Greg to make a duet, his own voice being actually stronger and better than Greg's. It was one of those songs that could go on indefinitely and certainly almost everyone in the hall seemed happy for it to do so as they sang and swayed and waved. In the middle of it Tom turned on one of his other lighting contraptions in addition to the swirling wheel and that was the footlights with their multi-coloured gels. The effect this created was enhanced by the lights being wired to come on severally and in sequence so that there was a constant movement of light that complemented the drama on stage and the surging music. At the end there was thunderous applause and cheering and stamping as Greg and the members of the band congratulated each other and got into lively conversation about what they might do next.

From then on the evening passed in something of a dazzle for the boys from the mainland, certainly for Johnny who had successfully re-encountered the girl he had started talking to at the beginning, Eva, and danced a lot with her as well as sharing another cigarette in El Capuccino. She obviously didn't have a boyfriend then. The mildly alcoholic fruit cup had run out by this time and they were down to lemonade but the party mood was firmly established and Johnny for one felt quite well away. He was not drunk but couldn't quite recall, reflecting on it later, how he came to be dancing not with the nice Eva who seemed set fair to become his partner for the rest of evening with possibly rewarding consequences, but with the girl with blonde hair who had initiated the swaying and hand-waving during Greg's song. She was certainly something, both in the gay abandon with which she threw herself into the proceedings and in looks, with regular features offset by the shortish blonde hair, some seriously crimson lipstick and a surprisingly tight single-piece black dress that revealed a lot of bare shoulder and top. Suddenly she said, 'Let's go outside and snog' – or that's what Johnny thought she said but she couldn't have, could she? It must have been 'smoke'. Anyway, she led him out of the room by the hand, and they were soon outside in the soft evening air. Duly Johnny offered her a cigarette which she accepted, wrapping her hand in his as he offered her a light. 'Let's walk on the cliffs,' she said, and taking his non-smoking hand in hers in an unself-conscious way, led him in that direction.

It was certainly a contrast that Johnny found very strange: inside had been noisy, crowded and very warm, whereas here they were alone in the fresh night, the distant ring of lights of Portsmouth twinkling on the other side of the black water. He suddenly felt vulnerable, uneasy and excited.

'Lovely, isn't it?' he said carefully, indicating the vista.

'You get a bit over-used to it,' the girl replied, drawing insouciantly on her cigarette, 'to be honest, I prefer London.'

'Is that where you live?'

'Sure do.'

'You know,' said Johnny, 'I don't know your name.'

'And I don't know yours. Fun, isn't it?'

Then quite before he knew what was happening and on no initiative of his own she had dropped her cigarette, stopped, turned round to face him and lifted her arms up over his shoulders, joining them behind his head. This was a signal not even Johnny could misinterpret. Putting his arms round her waist he leaned down and put his lips to hers. She moved in to him and extended her hands into his hair. 'Ummm,' she said as he drew gently away, 'worth repeating.' And she pushed herself yet more firmly against him so that he could feel the soft bulge of her breasts and kissed him again, this time, to his astonishment, putting her tongue into his mouth. It was a very long and very nice kiss, though Johnny was not at all sure about this tongue business or whether he was supposed to reciprocate. Drawing back a little after quite a prolonged contact, she said, 'Ummm, very tasty.' 'Really? What do I taste of?' Johnny replied hoarsely. Coffee and cigarettes couldn't be all that nice surely. She burst into a peel of laughter saying, 'Not tasty in that way, silly. I mean *you're* tasty.' Johnny didn't know what to say at all. 'That means you're good-looking,' she helped him, 'attractive.' 'Am I? You think so?' 'Of course, anyone would. My friend Inez saw you and said, 'Ooh, wouldn't mind a bit of that,' and I said, 'Hands off, he's mine.' ' Again she held up her lips to be kissed, closing her eyes. This time Johnny, emboldened by her compliment, put a bit more into it, including the insertion into her mouth of his tongue, so that now their tongues wriggled together in a way that could be very nice but was a bit odd and might take some getting used to. 'You're a funny one too,' she added as they broke apart again. 'Have you got a girlfriend?' 'Well, sort of.' 'You haven't done a lot of kissing before, have you?' 'No, not really, I suppose.' He'd have died sooner than admit the truth of it: that this was actually the first kiss of his life. 'Do you ever come to London?' she asked. 'No.' 'Pity. Let's go back.'

By the time they re-entered the theatre normal lighting had been resumed and packing up was in progress. 'Night, night,' she said and, lightly letting slip his hand, disappeared with a smile and a wave.

It was not until he was safely in his bed in the san where the visitors had been billeted that Johnny's feet, as it were, touched the ground. What the hell had happened? Well, it was quite obvious what had happened. He had been going along nicely with a pleasant girl and they were all having a good time when suddenly he was snogging a complete stranger on the cliff-top. It was incredible. How had it happened? Why had he done it?

'Hey, Angus, you awake?'

'No.'

'How'd you get on this evening?'

'All right, nothing special, had a good evening. Where did you get to?'

'Well, that's the incredible thing.'

'Oh God, not another drama. Keep it to the morning, OK.'

'All right.'

'On the other hand, let's hear about it.'

So Johnny told him. 'What's this thing with tongues?' he asked.

'God, you are an innocent, aren't you?'

'You mean it's normal practice, sticking your tongue in the other person's mouth and squirming it about?'

'Of course it is. It's called a French kiss.'

'Really?'

'Never heard of it?'

'Well... ' – in truth Johnny didn't think he had. 'French kiss, eh? Fancy that.' On reflection Johnny wasn't sure he did fancy it.

'Going to try and see her tomorrow?' Angus enquired.

'Yes. Yes, I should think so.'

'Slightly forgetting a certain person, are we? A certain publican's daughter?'

'No, of course not.'

'Well, supposing this one wants to write or see you again. Do you want to write or see her again? If so, what about Jane?'

'God, I hadn't thought that far. I suppose if I did that with whatshername and enjoyed it that must mean I don't really have the feeling for Jane that I thought I had.'

'Problem, eh?' said Angus, not without a little relish, as he turned over to go to sleep.

No, Johnny sought to persuade himself, not a problem. What this experience had told him was that his feelings for Jane, though very warm, were the feelings of a friend. Of course a friend who was a girl you would feel differently towards than you would towards a friend who was a boy. But that, clearly, was what she was: a friend. And that's what he was to her. Well, it stood to reason. If he could imagine spending the evening with another girl as he was sort of expecting to do with that nice girl Eva at the beginning with some possible nice cuddlesome consequences at the end of it, and if – on top of that – he was more than happy to go snogging with a different pretty girl, that quite clearly meant that his romantic and sexual interest was with them and not with Jane. So, no problem. Q.E.D.

'Well,' said Tom brightly at their cafeteria breakfast, 'have a good evening?'

How much did he know? 'Those lights were terrific,' Johnny replied evasively.

'Your bloke was terrific,' said Tom. 'He and Gordon – the singer – have really got together – working on a new number called *Rock Around the Block*.'

'Sounds promising.'

'They're going to form a new group – called the Gee Gees – and work on some new songs in the holidays.'

'Good.'

Then Tom grinned mischievously. 'I see the White Witch cast her spell on you all right.'

'Sorry?'

'The White Witch – Arabella. The girl you got some fresh air with.' The look on Tom's face made it clear that any evasion on Johnny's part would be pointless. 'I told you there might be some interest in you lot from the girls, didn't I? Arabella's not one to pass up an opportunity.'

'Yes, she's… quite a girl, isn't she?' said Johnny lamely. He suddenly realised that he didn't feel good about her at all, in spite of the intimacy of the previous evening. Come to think of it – because of that intimacy. And then he saw her, across the dining room. She saw him, smiled and waved and he instantly knew that it was nothing; that he felt nothing for her, that she felt nothing for him. That there was nothing to their relationship and no future to it. It was just a French kiss on the cliffs. That if they met again there might be more French kisses on cliffs but that they weren't really going to mean anything. That he had been a fool. That he had betrayed something good, and been disloyal. That he wished he hadn't done it.

Fielding remotely on the boundary later in the day was the time really to kick himself, for he was standing close to the very spot on which he had kissed Arabella. On the other hand, the beauty of the scene made it difficult for guilt and depression to flourish, for the cricket field seemed to be perched atop the cliffs, as if you could dive straight from third man into the sea, though in truth there was a considerable wooded slope and quite an extensive beach between the fielder and the water. There was full sun, a beautiful breeze and boats large and small, sail and steam, plying their way up and down the Solent, the immoveable Martello towers keeping guard in the roads.

Perhaps it was really best not to think about it. He'd decided anyway, hadn't he? that his relationship with Jane was that of friend and so there was no conflict between it and his attraction to sensuous blondes who put their tongues in your mouth. Why then, did his heart give a sudden lurch as he spied, sauntering around the boundary at some distance, a figure very like Jane's? If they were just friends he wouldn't for one thing be imagining someone who couldn't be there and for another his heart wouldn't lurch. So there was a problem.

Over ball. Move in to mid-on – no scope for daydreaming here. The opposing side were playing a careful game, their opening pair moving quietly into the twenties. The Worthingtonian assumption had been that because sport wasn't really all that important at this school they wouldn't have much of a team – hence the rather scratch side that had been sent across from the mainland, but perhaps that assumption had been arrogant. They would see.

Turning to make for his alternative position at third man, Johnny noticed that the imaginary Jane had made progress round the boundary and had now arrived alongside his position. He noticed also with another even greater lurch that the imaginary Jane was in fact not imaginary but Jane herself. She waved slightly as he approached.

'Jane!'

'Hi Johnny! Surprised to see me?'

'Not half !' Johnny was of course hardly in a position to conduct a continuous conversation, having to concentrate on the game, walk in and even occasionally chase a ball. But gaps between balls did offer opportunities.

'How's the game going?' she asked politely.

'Not got very far yet.' Crikey, what was to he to make of this? What was he to do? What was he to say? 'What are you doing here?'

'Revising.'

'Long way to come for a spot of revision.'

'Remember I said I had an aunt on the island? Well, I had Friday as a study day and Mum and Dad suggested I come over for a long weekend and concentrate on the revision instead of working in the pub.'

Johnny had his over at mid-on to digest this. She'd come

specially to the school because he was there. That meant something, didn't it? And she did seem quite pleased with herself. She also, Johnny couldn't help thinking, looked pretty as well, with her shiny dark hair, white sleeveless blouse and blue summer skirt. But her turning up now was more than a mite awkward. Why, she was practically standing on the very spot on which he and Arabella had…

'Don't let me distract you from the game,' she said, vaguely waving her French grammar as if to reassure him that she had her own resources. Perhaps she detected the uncertainty of his response. At any rate she had stopped smiling.

'No, right,' Johnny feebly replied, though events assisted him with a hotting up of the pace of the action as the opening batsmen pushed up the run rate and then one of them got out, to be replaced by a slogger who kept the outfield on their toes before being caught at deep mid-wicket. How was he going to play this one that had suddenly landed on his plate? Jane could well be around all day, she would expect to spend time with him when his side was batting and he wasn't in. What line was he going to take? Well, there was the grovelling confessional: Look, Jane, I'm really not someone you want to waste your time on – I'm really no good, unreliable, weak – if by any chance you were thinking of our… getting together I really feel you should think again, I'm not a good bet. Then there was the plain and hearty: Gosh, jolly friendly of you to turn up. Lovely here, isn't it? bla bla. That would certainly be the safer.

So that's what he did. After getting out at a fairly early stage for a modest score he was free to give her his full attention, so they sauntered over to a bench on the boundary. He was determinedly cheerful which seemed to brighten her up and they had a jolly conversation. She had an endless appetite for information about his school, every aspect of which she compared favourably with her own institution which she regarded as dull and second-rate, though she was a bit shocked by his account of the Latin lesson with Dr Cust.

'Do you mean a boy really was playing a mouth organ?'

'Only very quietly.'

'And you cheated with your translation?'

'Well, it's not cheating really. It's just getting a bit of help. Everyone does it.'

'It's not going to make you any better at Latin, though, is it? It's not going to help you pass A Level.'

'No, that's true, but there's no need to get serious about it in the Lower Sixth – plenty of time yet.'

Jane was wide-eyed with astonishment at this philosophy and her response did slightly make Johnny feel that maybe he wasn't getting the best out of the lessons. But that was Cust's fault. 'Anyway,' he added in a lame attempt to recover himself in her eyes, 'the Burk has made me go in for a prize.'

'What sort of a prize?'

Johnny had to explain about Speech Day and the guest speaker and the awarding of prizes in various subjects.

'Sounds a great day,' said Jane enthusiastically, 'what prize are you going in for?'

'Ancient History.'

'Do you think you'll win it?'

'Good God, no!'

'You don't sound very keen about it.'

'I'm not. I've been more or less bounced into it by the Burk.'

'Who's the Burk?'

'My tutor.'

'What's a tutor?'

'A member of staff who's supposed to take an interest in your work and you and so on. You have meetings with him.'

'On your own?'

'Yes, worst luck.'

'You mean it's just you and this member of staff talking about you?'

'That's right.'

'Gosh! sort of like a dad?'

'Well, I suppose in a way – we don't have our parents to

hand, you see.' The idea of the Burk as his dad Johnny found truly appalling.

What was more immediately appalling, however, was what Johnny now noticed. Approaching their point on the boundary was a small group of boys and girls – two of each in fact, though they were not evidently paired off – one of whom was unmistakably Arabella. Having seen and exchanged cheerful waves with her at breakfast, Johnny had not seen her since, and indeed, after what Tom had said about her, had not tried to do so. She was obviously a good-time girl and not at all the sort for him: French kissing of strangers and living in London was well out of his range.

But she wasn't going to let him off that lightly. As they drew alongside, chatting and laughing, Arabella said, 'Hello, Johnny – see, I found out your name.'

'Hello, Arabella.'

'Oh, you've found out mine – well, well. Enjoy the social?' she asked innocently, glancing at Jane. No one was introducing anyone to anyone.

'Of course,' Johnny managed, 'great music, great atmosphere.'

'Great company?'

'Sure.'

'Friendly girls?'

'Everyone was friendly.'

'You're pretty friendly yourself.'

Johnny was trying not to writhe but he was on the rack. Even he could see what Arabella was doing. There was a horrible contrast between the two girls: Jane, simply pretty, dark-haired, modest, thoughtful, ingenuous; and Arabella, blonde with model-y good looks, loud, arch, insinuating. And she hadn't quite finished. Her friends stood alongside her, impassive.

'Perhaps you haven't been to that kind of party before, Johnny. Learn anything?'

'What do you mean?' Johnny knew exactly what she meant

but he felt he was about to sink and could come up with nothing better.

'Oh, you know, what's the expression – birds and bees? Anyway, we mustn't keep you. Lovely spot this, isn't it – particularly by moonlight? See you in London maybe.' Arabella waved a vague hand with these words and she moved slowly on with her friends.

Johnny didn't dare look at Jane. He hadn't so much as glanced at her through that little exchange with Arabella. But he must. She was staring at the ground. She said nothing. Johnny said, 'That was one of the girls from the school. I... met her at the party last night.'

'So it seems,' Jane said, still not looking up. 'And what – ' she suddenly demanded, her little face now flaring up at him, 'and what, may I ask, did you 'learn' at the party?'

' 'Learn?' I didn't learn anything.' Johnny was taken aback: there was something in her face he'd never seen before – something white and fierce.

'Oh really? So what are Miss Blondey's 'birds and bees' that she's on about then?'

'She's a wild girl, says extraordinary things – you should have seen the way she carried on during Greg's song.'

'Oh, should I? Why?'

Johnny was in agony. Arabella had cut him to the heart, and in a completely different way Jane's words, her look and tone of voice, cut him to the heart too, and here he was trying to blather his way out of it. It was contemptible but he had to save himself.

'It was a very jolly party – very lively – one or two people maybe got carried away a bit.' Cowardly, pathetic. It wasn't even true.

' 'One or two' – including you?' Her voice was ice.

'Well, no more than a lot of people.'

'And I can see who you got carried away by,' said Jane, turning deliberately in the direction of the retreating party. Then she stood up. 'Well, I'm glad you enjoyed yourself and if you get a move on I expect you can catch her up – go on, see what more you can 'learn' from her.'

'Hey, hang on, Jane – don't be like that. That was a party, that was last night. What's that got to do with you and me and our friendship? Look, don't go... ' – for she was beginning to walk away. At his words she turned to face him and quietly echoed him: ' 'What's that got to do with me and you... ?' Well, if you can't answer that one, Johnny Clarke, you're more of a fool than I took you for. You can keep your friendship, I don't want it. I've got better friends and better things to do than...' – here her voice seemed to fail her and, turning her back on him once more, she walked hurriedly away, head down, and was soon lost to his bemused sight.

The Isle of Wight receded in their wake. Angus and Johnny sat on the outer deck at the stern, smoking, the Solent breeze whisking their exhalations away into the balmy evening.

'You don't really get the benefit, smoking in a wind, do you?' Johnny observed lugubriously.

'You, Clarke,' said Angus, gathering his repertoire of abuse, for Johnny had told him of the events of the afternoon, 'you, are a grade one arse-hole.'

'Am I ?'

'A gold-plated turd.'

'Perhaps you're right. I'm sure you're right. But why exactly? I mean, what have I done wrong?'

'What have you done wrong?! You mean apart from allowing yourself to be hooked by a tart and being unfaithful to your girlfriend, not to mention hurtful?'

'Well, hang on. Look, I know that Arabella thing was a bit – well, I was taken for a ride, wasn't I?'

'Well and truly.'

'OK, though I daresay you'd have taken advantage of the opportunity if you'd... ' –

'Not the point. It's *you* we're talking about. *You* did it.'

'OK. But 'unfaithful'? You can't be unfaithful to someone

unless you've got a relationship going, and we haven't.'

'Oh no? What's this letter-writing? *Scrabble*-playing?'

'We're friends.'

'Bollocks, you are. Tell me, why do you think she left in a huff? Why did she take on about you and the birds and the bees and Arabella? Eh? If you're just friends why did she react like that?'

'Well, I don't think... ' –

'No, you don't think, so I'll tell you: because she loves you, you stupid sod, God knows why but she is in love with you – that's 'love': L.O.V.E. She was horribly hurt to think of you carrying on with the blonde bit and she was mighty, mighty jealous.'

'Do you really think so?'

'Of course, it's obvious. Why should she come all the way to the Isle of Wight to see you if she didn't love you?'

'She didn't do that – she was in the Isle of Wight anyway.'

'Oh, come on! She knew you were going to the Isle of Wight, she wanted to see you so she comes – that thing about the aunt may well have been true but she went to stay with her in order to see you, not to have a revision week-end – which, incidentally, you have well and truly screwed up and if she fails her O Levels you can blame yourself. Right now she'll be weeping on her aunt's shoulder telling her about how her boyfriend's betrayed her with a tart and the aunt'll be telling her not to waste her time and trust on such a selfish and insensitive shit. Am I getting through to you?'

He was, oh yes, he was.

'Look at it this way – this is the test,' Angus went on. 'Picture Jane going back to her aunt's. Maybe a few friends – people Jane's age for company – come round, perhaps they go to the flicks, then on to the coffee bar, back home late. One of the lads stays on, they're on the sofa chatting, lights are low. He puts his hand on her knee, she looks up into his face and he bends towards her, her eyes close, she leans back, she's beginning to breathe heavily now, her lips part... ' –

'Shut up! I'll kill him! I'll kill *her!*'

Angus shrugged and flicked his fag end into the turbid waters. 'Now d'you get it?'

✴ CHAPTER 14 ✴

Reconciliation
on the Pier

In double Latin with Dr Cust on the following Monday morning – Johnny having spent his (gated) Sunday agonizing about Jane, writing letters to her which he then tore up, and attempting to make progress with his Ancient History project – Greg entertained the class with his mouth organ, quietly rehearsing *Rock Around the Block*, while Angus regaled Johnny with an account of his Sunday adventure at St Agnes.

He had finally broken through the barrier of Angela's illiteracy to arrange a meeting. He had (unlawfully) hitch-hiked to St Agnes, Chancton, to lurk in a small wood at the end of the school drive: they had to be very careful, Angela explained, or there would be trouble, since meeting boys was the biggest offence in the book. Anyway he had at last met her again and they had gone for a walk in the fields, which was very nice, though not – Johnny got the impression – attended by the same degree of physical passion as their first encounter. But it was not actually their meeting that Angus most wished to tell about – something else had happened.

'I was just coming out of the little wood to get on to the road so that I could hitch-hike back when what do I see but a familiar car just turning into the school drive. I know that car,

I say to myself – it's the Burkmobile!'

'No! He has taken up with that St Agnes mistress who came to the dance then?'

'Looks like it. She must be pushed, mustn't she?'

This piece of evidence, later discussed in the Waggery with the desultory cynicism of a weekday evening, was considered to be further evidence of the Burk's involvement in the Worthington girl operation. Initially hostile to the concept, the Lower Sixth had come to accept it as an historical inevitability, though they were bound to begrudge the ease with which their successors would be able to pursue their amours on site when they themselves had been confined to lengthy and unsatisfying letters, hitch-hiking miles for brief clandestine encounters, pedalling over the Downs on defective bicycles etc. This development was laying the axe to the venerable Worthingtonian tree they honoured and was not going to be of any benefit to them but it was now accepted.

'Do you realise that two years from now there will probably be girls in the Waggery?'

'Incredible!'

In Nick's study later, however, there was a lighter mood generated by the prospect of Speech Day and, following immediately upon it, the half-term holiday, short though that was. Speech Day was essentially a great bore but also relished as an opportunity to observe senior members of the establishment in their more pompous roles – there was formality, and processions and rarely seen worthies (the governors) and fatuous speechifying – 'Remember that general last year who spoke on the merits of Outward Bound?'

'They want shooting,' Billy opined morosely.

'Rather a crude fate, in my view,' Nick said. 'Something more drawn out, more ludicrous is called for.'

'Sabotage their braces and watch their trousers fall down,' suggested Angus.

'Low and impractical farce,' responded Nick drily. 'But if we consider some physical retribution for such vanity and self-importance let Johnny's girl administer some emetic in their morning coffee and see how they cope with an hour and forty minutes on the stage.'

'She won't be doing that,' said Johnny defensively. He did not, however, go on to say what she would be doing which a letter that morning had informed him.

While he had dithered over what to say to her or indeed whether he could write to her at all she had written to him. The envelope was ominously thin. 'Dear Johnny, I'm sorry I imposed myself on you at the cricket match at Clouds. Of course I should not have come. Clearly you have another life that does not include me and there is no point in writing any more or meeting. In fact I wouldn't have written this letter but I need to tell you that I shall be coming to your school Speech Day. The Bursar has invited us (Daddy and me) as his guests. I don't want you to think if you see me on that day that I am there because of you. Yours sincerely, Jane.'

Johnny's blood had run cold reading this: the shortness, the finality, the injured pride, the unspoken bitterness. What a fool he'd been – his silly escapade at Clouds had done for him in her eyes. He'd lost her and what had he got out of it? – a snog with a pretty girl who had no interest in or affection for him... whereas Jane... whereas Jane – well, just leave the word 'love' out of it and what had you got? To him a girl who obviously enjoyed his company, went out of her way to see him, took time and trouble to write to him and was hurt to think that he'd been kissing another girl. What more could a chap want? And he liked her – gosh, he did! He liked the look of her, her voice, the things she said, her eagerness, her sweetness, and he liked thinking of her. But: 'How could I really love her if I enjoy kissing another girl?' he had asked Angus. 'Kissing isn't the same as loving,' his friend had replied. 'Sex isn't love.' That was true, Johnny now realised. And in fact – and perhaps this was the test – now that he had lost her, what had he got? Just school and his friends. Before, they were enough, they were all he needed, but now they were not enough, they did not represent a reason for living. Her departure had drained the light and the life out of everything. That's how much she meant to him, whatever word he chose to label it with.

'Dear Jane, I was very sad to get your letter and I think I can understand why you don't want to have anything more to do with me after... ' – after what, exactly? 'after Saturday. I do not have 'another life' as you call it (except school, of course, which doesn't count) and I would really like to see you again if you are willing to meet me.' And here he went on to suggest a certain time and place in Bishopstown later that week before Speech Day – it being a saint's day, gating was suspended. This was not the love letter of the century by a long way but what he had done wrong he should not seek to put right by words on paper. It was time for action.

Naturally his first thought on arriving in very good time at the designated coffee bar was that she wouldn't come. She hadn't responded to his short letter, but then there'd hardly been time. Or maybe she simply was sticking by what she said and neither writing to him nor meeting him any more. Somehow he thought not. Angus had interpreted the letter as stemming from deep disappointment and hurt on her part, not an indifference to him. Perhaps then she hadn't got the letter. Perhaps – oh God! how fed up he suddenly was with all this bloody speculating: 'perhaps this', 'perhaps that', 'then again this' – it was so wearisome, it didn't get anywhere. When, oh when... ? – and she walked in.

She was in school uniform, of course, a rather shapeless blue mac over her blouse and skirt. It was a windy day and her dark hair was dishevelled. She tried to flick and push it back as she sat down opposite him. He wanted to take her beauty and her hurt straight into his arms but a look at her pale, tense face told him that wasn't the move to make. She was still a long way away. He was going to have to work hard if he was to win her back. Should he have brought flowers?

'Thanks for coming,' he said. Then he realised that while his heart was full he hadn't really planned what he was going to say.

'You had a good day at school?'

'Not bad.'

'So you're coming to Speech Day?'

'No.'

'You're not? I thought you said you… ' –

'I did, but I've changed my mind. I don't think it's a good idea.' She was cold, so cold, Johnny didn't know what to say.

'Oh.'

'I won't be coming to the school again – for any reason,' she added.

'I see… I see. That's a pity. Why?'

'Well – I've changed my mind… about several things. As I said in my letter.'

'Oh. Then why have you come here today?'

'To tell you myself, in person.'

'I see.' Johnny was lost. It was quite impossible, in the face of this implacability, to launch into his 'Look, I'm really sorry about the way I've behaved. I think you're great and why don't we… ' speech. Angus was wrong. Whatever she might be feeling, there was no doubt now she really didn't want to have anything further to do with him. Her pale face had shut against him. And yet, 'Would you like a cup of coffee?' he ventured. Playing for time. One last chance. Perhaps inspiration would come to him if he could just get away from that grim little figure that had replaced his chatty friend.

Staring gloomily at the machine built into the counter that was responsible for the creation of the particular variety of coffee on offer, Johnny had gone quite blank. The object of his vacuous gaze had all the chromium glories of the front end of an American limousine. Dwarfing its operator, it glittered and in action let out a harrowing screech as it delivered hot air or something through a nozzle into the jug of milk held up for it. The resulting beverage, topped with a tasteless froth that rapidly dwindled to a conventional ring of beige bubbles at the rim, was bitter and served in a shallow, small-handled cup that, once drained, retained some dark grains, not a few of which had inevitably and unpleasantly been swallowed with the last mouthful. And it suddenly seemed to Johnny that it just wouldn't do – all that performance for so little – all that sound and fury for a little cup of bitterness – it wouldn't do. So before the ordered drinks could be put in his hand he turned round with all the determination he was capable of to save the situation. And Jane's place was empty.

Johnny tore out of the coffee bar, looked desperately to right and left, sped off to the left, changed his mind and sped off to the right, crossed the road, stopped and again looked all around him. It was hopeless of course – how could he expect to see her amongst so many people? And if she was going to leave him like that – just walk out on him, having duly repeated, and in such bare and stony words, the dreadful message that she had expressed in her letter, she was going to make sure she got well away. And thus the reality hit him: he had seen the last of her.

The tension went out of him, his heart subsided and he found himself just drifting, sauntering down towards the sea-front for space and light and air and to be away from people. It was too late to try and find her now anyway, he realised, as she'd have made for the bus station – in the opposite direction. With the grand hotels behind him, Johnny strolled along a rather empty front, the wind from a dull sky whipping a grey sea into reluctant motion. It was high tide and the dirty water slopped at the steps. Gazing out to sea, Johnny yearned for the distance and emptiness of the horizon and almost relished the feeling of cold that began to drive into him. He made for the pier. Only a very few hardy souls were there, most of the amusements were empty, a few garish machines flashing their electric colours at no one. He leant on the rail.

He had failed. He had had a chance of a girlfriend – a good chance – and he had fluffed it. He had been keen and excited beyond imagining to begin with but in spite of her friendliness and encouragement he had failed to press his advantage, then got sidetracked by that silly business at Clouds and consequently blown it. She must be thinking something like:

Well, I thought he was nice but he turned out to be silly and shallow and pathetic, I'm better off without him. Oh for the vitality that had whizzed through him in those early days after having seen her; for the thrill of being beside her at the *Scrabble* board, for the excitement of slowly beginning to feel that something wonderful was happening. The old phrase, 'Nothing would ever be the same again', came into his mind not as a corny cliché but as a dreadful truth destined to stay with him all his life. He'd had a chance and he'd thrown it away.

'Johnny?'

He turned. It was her. Hands in the pockets of her mac to keep it from flapping, her hair blown half across her face. She joined him at the rail and they both looked down at the water. Soon their shoulders were touching and he felt the little flick of her hair in his face. She leaned gently into him until he felt the sweet soft pressure of her cheek against his. She turned to him: 'You cold?' she asked.

'Yes.'

He smiled and slipped both hands in through the gap in her mac and let his arms find their way around her waist and draw her gently towards his heart. Her hands came out of the pockets and met each other behind his head. They looked into one another's eyes. He put his lips to hers and kissed her – quite lightly, and slowly. Then she smiled and said, 'That's the first time I've been kissed.' He said, 'Well, it won't be the last,' and kissed her again. 'You've been crying,' he said, kissing a rivulet on her cheek. 'That's why I had to go to the loo,' she said. 'I couldn't let you see me crying, could I? You'd realise all those cold words were a complete lie.' 'You went to the loo? I thought you'd walked out on me!' 'I thought you'd walked out on *me*.' They laughed and he kissed the rivulet on the other cheek. 'I'm so sorry,' he said. 'What about?' 'I've been so... stupid. And I've handled everything so badly.' 'Oh, but I have too,' she replied eagerly. 'I've been so... silly and wrong and...' 'We're all right now, though, aren't we?' he said. 'Oh, we're all right all right,' she said and they laughed again. Then they

folded into each other and he said at her ear, 'You're so lovely.'
He could hardly breathe, hardly stand upright for her
loveliness. 'Got you now, have I?' he asked. 'Got me,' she
whisperingly replied. 'Don't let me go,' he said. 'Not a chance,'
was her answer and tightened her hold on him. He went on:
'Even if I'm silly and thoughtless and weak and all those things
I – well, the thing is, I love you.' She drew back sufficiently to
look at him and, smiling, closed her eyes as if to etch for ever
into the plate of her mind the picture of those words. 'And I've
never loved anyone else,' he added. 'I love you too,' she said,
so breathlessly she could hardly get out the words that he could
hardly hear.

And so they stood, clasped, the unheeded wind whipping off
a grey sea. And then what stories there were to be told...

❋ CHAPTER 15 ❋

Speech Day

Speech Day dawned with all the sunshine and expectancy of that normally pointless day. This day, though, was rather different, not just because Jane would be coming but because, as he discovered by a glance at the Headmaster's noticeboard on the way into breakfast, he had won the Ancient History Prize. This was a late award and added to the bottom of the typewritten list in the Wolf's distinctive purple ink. His heart lifted: Jane would see him collecting his prize. How proud she would be and how pleased he would be with her pride!

The prize-winners were seated separately from the other boys, parents and visitors who were crammed into Great Hall for an occasion that wags generally boycotted (unless they were themselves prize-winners). Proceedings conventionally began with a speech by the Wolf in which he detailed all the school's magnificent achievements, from Oxford and Cambridge scholarships to football victories. The boys of course knew most of this and didn't want to hear the rest, so Johnny, from his position of vantage, was avidly scanning the rows of visitors for sight of Jane – and incidentally his parents. For a while he was quite unable to find her, that small, dark-haired figure that he would pick out in a million, until he realised that that was her under a yellow hat – all the women wore hats. To Johnny, hats were a means by which even the most sensible women determinedly made themselves look ridiculous but that rule did not apply in Jane's case. He yearned towards her. He could hardly make signs at her but he stared and stared as intently as he could, sending great beams of love. He couldn't tell whether she was returning his gaze or not.

Since their union only two days before he had been unable to concentrate on anything else as, night and day, he recalled their every word and move. Stored in his memory was her body and her lips and the look in her eyes and her loving smile; and how she'd told him of the feeling that had suddenly come over her when they shared the washing up on Field Day; of the agonies in composing her letter; of how desperate she felt when, at Clouds, she thought he didn't care for her. Now he glowed with love and well-being. How on earth had he even managed to live without this feeling before?

'You will all know,' the Wolf's words now broke into Johnny's reverie, 'of the Governing Body's decision to admit girls into the Sixth Form in September year. I have now three further announcements to make regarding that decision. The first is that, although we have taken no steps as yet to advertise it, this new development in Worthington's history seems to have become very widely known already and my office has been inundated by telephone calls from interested parents, many of them under the mistaken impression that the first intake of girls is to be in the coming, rather than the following, September. In view of this extraordinary degree of interest – so strong as to amount to what I would almost term 'pressure' – the governors have decided to accommodate this demand by admitting a small number of girls on what might almost be called an experimental basis' (laughter) 'this very September. Numbering probably no more than a dozen, these girls will be accommodated in the school in certain quarters already decided upon, which – if they are not exactly purpose-built – have sufficient facilities as well as that necessary quality of segregation' (laughter) 'from the rest of the school. These quarters will be made ready in the coming holidays. Meanwhile our architects are about to submit plans for the construction of a brand-new, purpose-built house for the girls, to be ready – we fervently hope – by September year.

'The third decision,' the Wolf continued, glowing with self-importance and the rich satisfaction of a truly attentive audience so rare for a headmaster, 'regards the actual management of the house. To this vitally important post I am very happy to have made the appointment of Mr Derek Burkinshaw. Some of you may know that Mr Burkinshaw' – and here the Wolf's tone became arch – 'is a bachelor. Now I am authorised by the man himself to say' – here a meaning glance in the direction of the Burk, blushing and smirking in the staff rows – 'that by the time he takes up his duties Mr Burknishaw will no longer be in the unmarried state. This particular development – for which neither the governors nor myself may take any credit' (laughter) ' is a cause for congratulation on our part. I say we may take no credit but I am pleased to relate that the Mrs Derek Burkinshaw-to-be was first encountered by her future husband in this very room on the occasion of the annual dance with St Agnes. And what's more, the future Mrs B., who is at present a member of staff at that school, brings with her – as a dowry, you might say – experience of the care of girls which will be invaluable to her husband. In short, I am sure we wish Mr Burkinshaw the greatest happiness in the management of all his girls!' (Laugher and extensive applause.)

There was little time to reflect on the implications of these announcements as the guest-of-honour now presented the prizes. Johnny was more nervous than proud during the moments of his individual part in these proceedings but he did think of Jane watching him as he shook hands, received his book and returned to his seat to the sound of applause: some of that was her hands clapping, he thought. It was the first prize he had won since prep school and actually, he reflected, as the guest of honour praised the prize-winners for their efforts, he owed the winning of the prize to the Burk – not just for awarding it but for virtually having made him go in for it – and also to Jane for having taken an interest that had definitely spurred him on.

By good chance it was Jane and Mr Baxter that Johnny ran into leaving Great Hall, rather than his parents. It seemed to be all Jane could do not to throw herself round him in the cloisters. She was glowing with delight as she said, 'Why didn't you tell me?'

'Tell you what?'

Jane pointed at the impressive tome in Johnny's hands. 'That you'd won a prize.'

'I didn't know.'

Mr Baxter congratulated him too.

Johnny stood there in his suit, feeling embarrassed, but Jane was looking beautiful in her yellow dress and little matching hat. He wouldn't be able to tear himself away from her for a moment. And that was a problem because what about his parents? He had been characteristically hoping that events would sort things out for him. Ah! here were his parents. Johnny introduced them. They of course had no idea who these two other people were or any inkling that their son would gladly have sacrificed the entire half-term holiday with them for half an hour with Jane, and were therefore uncertain in their small talk but congratulated their son on his prize. The introductions and initial chat over, Mr Baxter announced to Johnny's sudden alarm that they must be off.

'Aren't you staying for lunch?' Johnny asked desperately.

'No,' Mr Baxter replied. 'I've already had to turn down the Bursar's kind offer. I must be getting back to work.'

'Can't you stay and share our picnic?' Johnny tried to make the words sound more like an invitation than a plea. To his relief and delight it was quickly arranged that though Mr Baxter must go Jane would stay and join them in their lunch. Mr Baxter's offer to collect Jane later in the afternoon was converted by Johnny into an offer on their part to drop Jane off on their way home for the half-term holiday.

Delighted with these arrangements and his own masterly hand in making them, Johnny did not reflect on any unease that might have been felt by his parents at being obliged to stretch their picnic – indeed their whole afternoon – to accommodate a completely strange girl whom they were also expected to take home. Daring the occasional touch of the hands with Jane (readily reciprocated with a glance and a smile) as they went, Johnny led them all to their car on the River Field where they tucked into their picnic. Johnny was relieved that Jane got on famously with his mother and father but he realised as they talked that some of half-term might have to be spent in explaining to them what the nature of his relationship with Jane was, how it had come about and so forth. It was certainly going to require rather more editing than the information passed to parents generally involved. Both his mother and father had shot him the occasional strange look as if they were contemplating their son anew and not entirely without apprehension.

After the picnic Johnny abandoned his still somewhat bewildered parents to the dubious pleasure of watching the First Eleven in action against the MCC and set off smartly with Jane in order to have her all to himself. She was delighted with his parents, delighted with the day, delighted especially with his prize which, with its stiff covers and special Worthington College Prize bookplate calligraphically inscribed with his name and achievement, she couldn't get over. And she was delighted with the school. Given her way, she would have seen it all from end to end; even as it was, in the course of the afternoon Johnny traversed more of the college than he would in a normal week, entering at Jane's eager request into rooms of no conceivable interest, including some whose door he had never darkened in his three years at the place. The science laboratories proved especially enticing to her and she watched with avid absorption the various experiments that were being demonstrated for the enlightenment of parents. To Johnny the evil smell of a chemistry lab, the stained benches and the glass-stoppered bottles ranged along them with their formulae printed on their sides brought back such fresh memories of fumbling incompetence with Bunsen burners in his early days in the school that he felt quite sick. She even insisted on visiting the classroom off the library in which the infamous Monday morning Latin lessons took place.

'Gosh!' she exclaimed radiantly, 'what facilities! You're so lucky to have done Science in labs like that.'

'Lucky!' Johnny made no comment.

Thrilled though he was to be with her, Johnny was under some restraint with Jane as he went about the school. It being Speech Day, of course there was nothing at all remarkable about being accompanied by a girl and with a bit of luck anyone who wondered about her identity would assume she was Johnny's sister. Although he delighted in their little opportunities for physical contact there could be no out-and-out hand holding such as they had established as their normal practice in Bishopstown not two days before and Johnny's hand felt empty and pointless without hers. But they had to visit his study too, of course – she was especially keen to see that: 'So that I can imagine you at school,' she said – and there they sat holding hands, though not for long so eager was she to see and to touch almost everything in his room.

As they sauntered down the drive to rejoin his parents at the cricket field she breathed in the whole place and sighed out – 'I do envy those girls coming in September.'

It had not hitherto occurred to Johnny to make any connection between those girls eligible for admission to Worthington and anyone he himself might know. The idea that Jane herself might be one – as indeed theoretically she might now that the first girls were due to enter the school the next term – was quite new and quite startling.

'But I don't suppose,' she continued, 'that there's any hope of it – Dad couldn't afford it.'

'Perhaps they'll do scholarships,' said Johnny, to be encouraging. Actually the truth was he didn't feel as keen on the idea as Jane did.

'She's a nice girl, Jane,' remarked Johnny's mother as they settled for the drive home, having dropped Jane off at the Rose and Crown. She and Johnny had agreed on another meeting on the pier which they had decided was a good place for them. That would be on the Tuesday, so Johnny was not so miserable at leaving her when he had the prospect of seeing her again in three days. Nothing else mattered now. Even the half-term break – normally something to be looked forward to and relished – was of little appeal since it must be spent without her. He would get a letter off to her on Sunday, she'd get it on Monday, so...

'Yes,' Johnny replied unencouragingly. Being alone in the back of the car saved his blushes from observation, which was a relief. So should he tell them more? Parents were like swans in swimming quietly up alongside you, implicitly appealing for bread. The trouble was that the more crumbs you dished out the more persistently they pursued you in hope of more. On the other hand, if he could be evidently controlling the supply, they might take the hint and drift off. So he gave them the basic facts about her: the most basic fact of all – that they loved one another – was not, however, one of them.

❋ CHAPTER 16 ❋

A New Future
for Jane

The best thing about half-term was writing to Jane, though it was good to eat proper food and not have to get up in the morning. It was also a pleasure to wear your own clothes instead of school uniform. How much better it would be, he thought, if Jane lived near his home instead of his school and then they could enjoy more time together, away from masters and gating and exams. Perhaps she could come to stay: would his parents allow that?

Then back to school and a detailed dissection of the Wolf's tri-partite announcement about girls on Speech Day. That they would actually be coming the very next term was most startling, bringing the girl question out of the realms of the theoretical into one that closely affected them all. It was no longer a matter of opposing on principle an innovation that would not actually touch them, but a matter of sorting out their attitudes to the prospect of sharing their lives with girls. Though few, the girls would undoubtedly be there, if not in the classes of their year-group or of course in their houses, then in the dining-hall, in chapel, in assembly, walking about the place, and exchanging the common currency of school life. Could girls be members of the Waggery? What uniform would they wear? What would be the rules about boy/girl relationships? Would hand-holding in public be permitted, as at Clouds? Would there be Saturday night socials, as at that place? Would the girls be boy-hungry or playing hard to get, there being so few of them? Would the boys of the Upper Sixth – themselves next year – deign to have anything to do with them? It was well known that girls preferred boys older than themselves so perhaps a bit of deigning on the part of Johnny and his friends, they decided, might not be too infra-dig.

The decision regarding first-year accommodation for girls was the one that concerned those who so frequently met and entertained each other there and especially the one who considered it his home: Nick had already, after the unmistakably significant visit of the Burk, adjusted himself to the fact that its future would not continue beyond his own tenure of a year and a bit. Now, however, that he would be discommoded; now that he had to accept that this was his last term there; that in September he would have nothing better than an eight-foot-by six-foot box in the breezeblock annexe, Nick was in arms.

'It's the only thing that makes life at all bearable,' he lamented one evening as the four gathered for a nightcap in his rooms. 'How will Luigi care for me in that battery-hen box you characters consent to live in? And how would I be able to entertain you? How can I stay in bed till eleven in the morning if I have to sleep – God help me! – in a dormitory?' And so he went on. There was, of course, no consolation to offer: it was a very bleak situation.

'It's the Burk you have to thank for it,' put in Billy.

That character duly came in for the range of contemptuous abuse that was customarily heaped upon him when his name cropped up.

'I'm sure it was him who picked on these rooms for the girls – mean sod!'

His forthcoming engagement was derided as a shallow expedient designed to secure him the prestigious position to which he had been appointed. In a spirit of unpractical vindictiveness, various vile reprisals were imagined and dramatised in conversation, but even Nick was helpless. Billy fuelled his rage with tempting images of retribution, referring to certain inhumane practices, prevalent, he assured them, in some of the less developed areas of his own country that would have seemed excessive in England and must therefore not be contemplated; poison, incantations, knives and fire figured prominently in these. Putting sugar in the petrol tank of his car, persuading his pupils to join in a relentless campaign of sounding all their b's plosively, making discreet but obscene gestures at any girls who presented themselves for consideration – such recourses were canvassed but not pursued and left to expire as the hot air of impotent rage. They just had to lump it.

'What about the old buffer in the bog at your club you were talking about?' suddenly suggested Angus. 'He seemed to have some sort of goods on the Burk. Maybe you could get some more out of him.'

This seemed at first to be quite a promising line. But the fact that Nick did not know the old buffer's name and could not guarantee to re-encounter him at the club ruled it out as a possibility.

'It's an attractive idea, though,' Nick said. 'Somewhere behind the buffer's gossip lies the Burk's Achilles heel. But without access to that heel direct confrontation with him on his own ground is bound to end in his success and our humiliation.'

Their discussion was at this point interrupted by shouts from outside.

'It's the yobbos!' cried Angus with glee, dashing out of the room and leaping into the bedroom – Nick's spare – that commanded a view of the path up which the shouters would be passing. It seemed they were more in noisy high spirits than intent on the destruction of windows or the provocation of inmates but Angus could not resist hurling out a facetious aspersion of the manliness of the members of the Bishopstown football team which the yobbos might be assumed to support.

'Avaunt, curs!' added Nick in his most patrician tones while Billy's contribution was an exhortation to unfurl the banner of revolution and strike a blow for the oppressed proletariat.

These expostulations were greeted with further vocal execrations from the passing youths, shouts substantially composed of obscenities. The visitors were not, however, disposed, or perhaps just not equipped, for any more tangible response to the Worthingtonian provocation and, without a stone thrown, drifted on their nonetheless noisy way down the hill.

'Of course, it just shows,' said Nick, as they resumed their comfortable seats in the sitting room, 'that these quarters are distinctly vulnerable. Has the Burk thought of that? Has he taken into account the dire possibility of hordes of proletarian youth threatening the precious innocence of his charges? A sexual assault would not get his cause off to a good start.'

But while the Nick-and-Billy half of the company moved into a dissatisfied phase, the Johnny-and-Angus half were rather happy. Angus had made a satisfactory arrangement whereby he and Angela were continuing to meet almost as often as Johnny and Jane. Angela had not, Angus had to admit, much intelligence, but apart from continuing to bestow her ample physical favours (up to a point) she did have, Angus asserted, a charming personality. Johnny and Jane, after the difficulties of the earlier stage of their relationship settled down now to a steady hand-holding level, though the kiss of their first declaration had not been repeated, as if so wonderful and precious an exchange should only be made at moments of the most intense feeling. He loved her and he had told her so, she ditto, and they were very happy together. Not that they were often together, however, for although Johnny's period of gating was now expired the combination of his cricket and Jane's endless revision for O Levels left very little free time, particularly in view of the distance between them. They wrote often and intimately and at length but more about each other's doings and feelings than protesting their affection. They now began 'My dearest… ' – a little phrase which when he both wrote and read it sent Johnny into a trance of devotion – and ended 'With Much Love… ' but made no declarations.

They did meet again on the pier and they wrapped themselves happily round one another as they stared down at the jinking water and out to the horizon. They talked of the holidays: they would go to France; they would go on a cycling and camping tour of the Lake District; Johnny would come and work in the pub and mow the lawn and they would go for endless walks on the Downs. There was so much they might do – not that it mattered what they did as long as they were together; even revising for his beastly Maths was a pleasure because Jane could help him with it.

Then one day Jane's letter – they wrote every day even on the days they met – said, 'I've got a bit of news – good news, for me anyway – but I'll tell you more when we meet.' Which they did at what they called 'Halfway House', which was not a house at all but a track leading deep into the Downs. They hid their bicycles in the gorse – Erf had been duly squared on receipt of reparations for the damaged gears – and walked along the track carrying the picnic tea Jane had brought. Soon the small talk dried up as Jane's excitement and Johnny's apprehension collided to bring them to the point: what news? Well, she must tell him but she wasn't sure how he would take it so she was a bit nervous. What was she on about? He dropped her hand.

'Well… ' she began, taking a deep breath.

'Well?'

'Oh – it's so difficult to say.'

'Just say it!'

'All right. OK. I'm coming to Worthington in September. There – now I've told you. Oh! I do hope you're not going to be unhappy about it. It's the best thing I can think of… it's not absolutely certain, of course, I mean I haven't been accepted yet but Dad's spoken to someone at the school and he said with my record and O Level prospects I should be all right.' She was rattling on to keep him from having to say anything before he was ready and to overwhelm with her enthusiasm any initial reservation he might have. 'When my exams are over I've got to go and have one or two tests and interviews and things. I'm so excited... but what do you think?' she glanced up at him nervously. 'You haven't said anything.'

'Haven't had much of a chance,' he replied, smiling wanly. 'Well, of course, I think that's great.' In fact Johnny did not yet know what to think but he did not want to disappoint Jane or spoil her excitement.

'We would see each other every day,' she beamed.

'Yes. Um, I thought you said your Dad wouldn't possibly be able to afford it.'

'Well, apparently that's been made all right somehow – I don't know how. So a week tomorrow I'm going with Mum and Dad to the school and we're going to have a look round and meet Mr Burkinshaw and he'll tell us all about it. Of course,' she added, 'I know you and your friends don't like Mr Burkinshaw.'

'Oh, well... ' – Johnny attempted some reassurance, not least in view of the man's virtually setting him up for the Ancient History Prize – 'I expect he's different to girls.'

'I'm so grateful to Dad,' Jane enthused. 'It's such a lovely way to launch me on my A Levels.'

'Yes,' Johnny agreed, though it was not customary to regard the Lower Sixth year at Worthington in such a light but rather as a well-merited period of recuperation after O Level and a recharging of batteries before the true demands of A Levels which might make themselves felt at some time during the summer term in which they were to be taken. With such a keen attitude, would Jane be suited to the school? How would she fit in to his existing life? Would she become a member of the company? He simply couldn't picture it.

After their picnic they lay on their backs on the grass cropped short and firm by the sheep, holding hands and looking up at the sky.

'Yes,' he said, 'we'll see each other every day. We won't be in the same classes or year group but we'll be bumping into each other all the time around the place.'

'And we'll spend all our free time together,' added Jane eagerly.

'I'm not sure you'll have much,' teased Johnny, 'what with being so keen about work and your netball and music and everything. And you'll want to make friends with the other girls too.'

'Yes,' Jane agreed, ' that'll be important.'

What Johnny couldn't yet say out loud was his apprehension that she, along with the other girls, would attract a lot of attention and comment from the boys. Did she realise this? He would probably have to overhear comments about her. 'What do you think about the little dark girl? – what's her name?' 'Jane Baxter, I think. Hmmm, not bad, bit skinny, small tits. Wouldn't kick her out though.' Was Jane aware how frankly crude boys could be about girls? Did she really want to expose herself to that kind of comment? Did she want him to have to hear it? And then there was the more important fact that she was his girlfriend, and he wanted to keep it that way. She wasn't going to have her head turned by anyone else who started fancying her, he felt sure, but she wouldn't be used to having all these boys around, some of whom were pretty smart operators, and who knew what might happen? Well, no use getting twitchy about it. He was glad that Jane was coming to Worthington but he couldn't help being a little apprehensive.

She wondered about his silence. 'You don't think I'll start taking an interest in the other boys, do you?' she said, as if divining his thoughts.

'Well, they'll certainly be taking an interest in *you*,' Johnny replied a little bleakly.

'That doesn't mean I'm going to take an interest in *them*, does it?'

'No.'

'Well, then… '

'Well, then what?'

'Well, then you don't have any reason to be… to… –

Johnny, don't you trust me?'

'Yes, of course I do but I think maybe you don't realise…'
He too trailed off.

'Realise what?' she persisted gently.

'Jane,' he said, sitting up and looking into her face, 'do you
think we'll be holding hands in a year's time?'

She looked amazed. 'Well, of course I do.' She too sat up to
meet his gaze. 'Why ever not? What do you mean – don't *you?*'
She looked alarmed now.

'Oh, yes, I do, I do,' he hastened to reassure her, 'but aren't
you ever afraid that… I mean, don't you ever wonder… ?'

She looked back at him. Words failed them both. Johnny
leant forward a little and softly kissed her unmoving lips. After
a moment she said quietly, 'No, I'm not afraid and I don't ever
wonder and if you think that I am going to be… to be
unfaithful to you when I get to Worthington then I have only
one thing to say.'

'What?'

For answer she took his head gently in her hands and,
closing her eyes, kissed him softly and long on the lips. 'That,'
she said.

Johnny almost fainted.

❈ CHAPTER 17 ❈

Juvenile Offenders

It was not long after this that school routine was varied by the visit of the Borstal lads. This was an innovation mentioned by the Wolf in his opening speech of term as one of the indications of the school's new openness to the outside world, and involved half a dozen boys of school age whose own Borstal routine was varied by the experience of three days in a rather different, and yet in some ways very similar, institution.

Johnny and the other eleven hosts (each Borstal boy being shared between two Worthingtonians) awaited their arrival with some trepidation. By virtue of his father's work in the parish Johnny had some knowledge of the youth of the working classes with whom his parents urged him to mix for the good of his soul, but he had no direct relations with what might be called juvenile criminals. What these lads had done to be detained at Her Majesty's pleasure was not known, but Johnny supposed it was things like stealing on a modest scale, shoplifting, perhaps the odd breaking-and-entering, vandalising council property, perhaps even as bad as assaulting old ladies.

It was not easy to imagine the six youths who climbed self-consciously out of their unmarked blue minibus as violent criminals or indeed threats to society at all. Indeed one or two of them looked as if the only crime they would be capable of was being manipulated by stronger criminal personalities and then getting caught, though another one or two had a hefty and threatening look to them in Johnny's eyes. They were dressed remarkably like naval cadets, their top halves being clothed in ordinary battledress of a dark blue colour, and they were totally monosyllabic in communication.

Somewhat to everyone's surprise, Nick had volunteered to participate in this visit. He argued that since they were of the lower and criminal class the lads with whom they would be dealing would almost certainly be more intelligent, more interesting and better-natured than the bourgeois dullards with whom he was daily surrounded. How Nick might be supposed to manage a return visit, when (in the holidays) the hosting Worthingtonians went for a few days to the Borstal, Johnny could not imagine. Nick's response was that by all accounts these institutions were immeasurably superior in their facilities and amenities to those provided at Worthington. Indeed the previous year's visitors from the school had talked with awe of the spaciousness and modernity of the Borstal lads' accommodation, of the cubicles in the dormitories that were large and enclosed enough almost to be termed rooms. These included a wardrobe, on the inside of the doors of which they stuck pictures and posters. The Worthingtonians talked of a room fitted with several rows of cinema seats in which television and films could be watched. They were even allowed to smoke.

The contrast between the two institutions was soon further established as unfavourable to Worthington by the Borstal boys' response to the food. They were awed by the grandeur of the dining hall, with its lofty timbered ceiling and august portraits of former headmasters, and impressed by being waited upon, though they were astonished that this menial task should be performed by boys whose parents were paying large fees for the privilege. But they were appalled by the quality of the food and incredulous at the absence of choice. Their soft cods' roe on cold fried bread went uneaten. Although Johnny's intention had been to fasten on the least offensive-looking of the Borstal lads as his personal charge, Nick, his partner, had determined otherwise and seized upon a glowering oaf. This person's opinion of the food was metaphorical and obscene so that when Johnny took him after the meal to Nick's rooms Nick was able to strike just the right hostly note by providing him with an enormous dish of spaghetti bolognaise that Luigi had prepared. The lad, whose name was Steve, thawed rapidly under the influence of this unexpected treat and the easy friendliness with which Nick engaged him in conversation. Johnny left them for cricket practice with the uncomfortable but grateful feeling that Nick – as usual – had the whole situation more in hand than he had.

The Borstal lads did not attend lessons, their own academic education having come to an end some time previously, so various practical and recreational activities had been laid on for them instead. Most of these Nick, with almost no lessons of his own to call him away, attended, even if only in a spectatorial role, with the result that he was swiftly identified by the visiting party as the bloke who knew what was what. Amongst them the title of 'squire' was generally conferred with mostly mock deference on anyone of even modest bourgeois status but Nick was addressed as 'sir' and without a hint of irony. Substantial meals were reserved for Steve alone, a privilege that transformed that lad's seeming malevolence into an instant and intense loyalty to his benefactor. But liquid refreshment he liberally offered to all the visitors so that within thirty-six hours of their arrival Nick's room had become their centre and Nick their leader.

It was while taking their ease during the necessarily quiet hour of prep that the local lads once more happened to make their raucous passage down the back path. Unfriendly exchanges between town and gown had been increasing of late but so far there had been no real violence. Though peacefully content with coffee, beer and cigarettes, the Borstal boys roused as one at the provocative sounds from outside the window and leapt to points of visual vantage all agog for action should the opportunity arise and their leader give the order. When one of the passers-by made an unmistakably obscene suggestion they burst forth in a rich if unorchestrated chorus of abuse. The passers-by must have been intimidated by this unusually robust response for they moved rapidly on. Nick was smiling, no doubt at the thought of the puzzlement of the youths on hearing such convincingly proletarian accents from members of what they knew to be a 'toff' opposition.

Steve was not so amused. ' 'Oo them buggers, sir?' he demanded, his cheeks flushed with anger and frustration.

'Oh, just local chaps going about their lawful business,' Nick replied artfully.

'Lawful!' Steve's tone was one of righteous indignation. ' 'Oo do they think they are, using language like that in a place like this? Ain't they got no respect?'

Nick continued to play down their offensiveness while conveying the (false) information that on a previous occasion it had involved the breaking of Nick's bedroom window. The further information that no reprisals had been taken against them incensed Steve and one or two of the others to a high pitch of violent intention.

'We'll get out and do 'em,' he incitingly suggested.

'I mustn't allow you to break school bounds,' Nick calmly riposted.

'Bugger bounds,' said Steve, but was nervous evidently about acting on his bold words. At which point one of the mousier-looking lads unexpectedly piped up with, 'I expect my bruvver's one of 'em.'

'Your brother?'

'Yeh, I live near 'ere – in Bishopstown.'

'Do you really?' Nick seemed excessively interested in this information and gave his attention to the speaker in a highly confidential manner.

Johnny retreated to his study. It was all very well for Nick to spend the whole evening with the lads – he hadn't got any work to do. He certainly hadn't got O Level Maths to take in two days' time and also he wasn't in love. Johnny re-read Jane's letter that had arrived that day, partly of course for the sheer love of her, partly to try and make sense of the Maths in it that was in response to a query he had made in his last letter. The day after tomorrow was their big day, the day of his O Level Maths, Jane's visiting the school now that she had finished her exams and – best of all – an agreement to meet at Halfway House in the evening. Johnny could only manage an hour after prep with any safety but that was better than nothing. Since the last kiss his own emotional temperature had risen, which he would not previously have thought possible. He replayed it – them, rather – time and time again, though as each time he did so their glory became fainter. He knew that those kisses were not the most passionate or professional ever delivered but he was not critical. The wonder and the beauty of the feel of her lips as he kissed them were beyond anything he could think of. And the way she had so gently taken his head in her hands and closed her eyes to kiss him – well, he almost swooned remembering it. He could hardly wait for them to meet again and kiss again.

With such memories and such prospects of love and happiness an hour passed pleasantly. Then, a little guilty at abandoning his hostly responsibilities to his partner, he went to call on Nick before going to bed. The lads had been claimed by their own hosts and taken off to their sleeping quarters, leaving Nick and Steve alone. The latter, exhausted after a day rich in sensual comfort and excitement, had gone to sleep, fully dressed, in one of the spare rooms. Nick himself was musing.

'Well, they enjoyed the visit from the yobbos,' Johnny observed.

'Didn't they?' Nick's eyes lit up. 'I think we could have a little fun, there, you know.'

'Are you plotting something, Nick?'

'It is an opportunity, isn't it?'

'What for exactly?'

'Well, as I was saying the other day, if it could be established that these rooms were vulnerable to violent interference the school might have to change its mind about their suitability as accommodation for these precious girls.'

'And you might be able to keep them?'

'Exactly. And thwart the Burk at the same time.'

'Well, don't let Steve know about your gun – I think he could get silly ideas, that one.'

'My gun? I have still got it here, haven't I? Look under the chesterfield, would you, Johnny... Ah, yes, I have indeed. Well now... ' and he let that train of thought fade away and picked up another. 'And what's more, it transpires that one of our lads has some family connection locally. Now if I can get him to stir up a little more aggressive spirit amongst them and we have some idea of when they might strike we could be prepared for them.'

'Have a bit of a battle, you mean?'

'Something along those lines, yes.'

'Could be trouble.'

'Would be trouble – and some of the responsibility for it must fall upon the ample shoulders of our guests,' Nick deftly countered. 'They're used to it, after all.'

Johnny was not comfortable with the direction that Nick's thoughts were obviously taking so he left him to follow them on his own. Why join in making trouble, he thought, when he had Jane to love?

❊ CHAPTER 18 ❊

Trouble – and an Accident

Johnny had kept a record of his answers in the O Level Maths paper and this he brought with him to their next rendezvous at Halfway House. He felt he had done quite well and looked forward to Jane telling him so.

He was to be disappointed: not in her assessment of his mathematical performance (which never got a look-in), but in her mood. For a start she was late and his heart had begun to sink as she did not appear, but she pedalled up at last rather breathlessly and although she was evidently glad to see him he instantly noticed a gloom about her that rather worried him. It wasn't like her.

'Did you enjoy your visit to the school?' he enquired carefully, as they headed along the track. 'How did you like Mr Burkinshaw?'

'Yes, I did,' she replied, 'but Mum seems to have taken against it rather. Or him.'

'Oh?'

'Of course she hadn't been to the school before and me coming in September was all Dad's idea – and mine, of course. She just sort of went along with it. But she got all frozen during the visit and since then – you know, discussing it – she's been very unencouraging.'

Johnny would have been inclined to say he wasn't surprised at a mother hesitating to hand her daughter over to the tender care of the Burk, but the case was rather too serious for that. Her mother had seemed to Johnny a slightly background figure, though friendly and obviously quite happy about the boy her daughter was 'seeing', but at home she was eclipsed by Mr Baxter's lively personality. It was clear from this, however, that she was obviously a serious force in the family.

'The interview with Mr Burkinshaw was rather awkward,' Jane went on. 'He took us up to his room at the top of the Tower and gave us tea – fantastic number of books he's got – and Dad asked all sorts of questions but Mum, who usually has something to say, hardly said a word. And Mr Burkinshaw seemed a bit awkward, too, I thought.'

'And since then Mum has been unencouraging?'

'Yes.'

'What does she say?'

'Didn't like the atmosphere... wasn't sure that the school was really ready to take on girls... why hadn't we been shown where the girls were going to live? – that sort of thing.'

Johnny thought Mum had a point or two there but didn't say so.

'But it was more than that, it wasn't so much what she said as the way she was... just negative.'

'Perhaps she hadn't realised before that it meant you living away from home. She'll miss you. Still, I expect she'll get used to the idea, if you carry on being keen and Dad supports you.'

'Yes, but it isn't like her. She's always been so anxious for me to do well, me being an only child and all that – telling me that just because I'm a girl doesn't mean I can't do as well as boys. You'd think she'd be all in favour of me having the opportunities of Worthington – and doing better than all you lazy boys.' She managed a smile to end with.

'Maybe she thinks you'll be distracted by all us 'lazy boys'. '

'I just don't feel happy about it. I'm not going to go ahead with it unless she comes round.'

'Shame to spoil your end-of-exam happiness,' said Johnny, and tried to cheer her up, with little success. It was a lovely evening but it was wasted on them. He kept quiet about the Maths paper.

Before going to bed that night Johnny called on Nick. Billy was not officially a host but he was occasionally around, though the lads regarded him with some suspicion, most if not all of them never having met a black person before. To them he was something of an enigma since black people were at best 'natives' in the popular mind if not downright 'niggers' and here was a darkie as one of the toffs. Billy did not help by keeping his inscrutable counsel.

'Any action with the yobbos?' Johnny enquired.

'No, that's tomorrow night,' Nick replied.

'How do you know?'

'Oh, we've got it all arranged – you know, through the weasely boy whose brother lives in Bishopstown. I managed to organise a visit for him today and he's set it all up. It seems they're going to come in some numbers, and armed to boot, so it could be interesting.'

'Armed! Bloody hell! Armed with what?'

'We shall see – but we shall be ready.'

'What preparations have you made then?'

'Well, there's ourselves, of course. Johnny – you will be in during prep tomorrow, won't you? – and the lads.' He signalled in the direction of the somnolent Steve. 'They'll be in the forefront. I've managed to rustle up an air-gun and a couple of catapults belonging to Luigi's chums so while we're having a little last evening party for the Borstal lads down here tomorrow night there should be interesting developments.'

'You're not going to use the shotgun, are you?'

'Only for its sound effect – and anyway the school authorities will assume it's part of the enemy's armoury, not ours. Steve's going to position himself in the hedge on the other side of the path before the attack and then give them a fright from the rear.'

'Christ! Do you trust him?'

'No, not a bit.'

'All sounds bloody risky to me, Nick.'

'Don't worry, Johnny, the Burk's the one who's going to suffer – not us.'

Feeling uneasy at the whole idea, Johnny concentrated on thinking about Jane. For himself he didn't much care, he decided, whether Jane came to Worthington in September or not. In many ways the present arrangement was as good as having her on the spot. For one thing they met reasonably often and in private, which was important and might be more difficult at school where any couple seen heading for a place of privacy would come under immediate suspicion. But she was obviously keen to come and he felt sorry for her as she was so dispirited by her mother's inexplicable resistance to the idea. It all depended, Johnny reckoned, on how persuasive Mr Baxter could be. Surely with his support Jane would get her way.

Johnny was of course not to know that coincidental with the moment he put his head on the pillow that night a certain aged Dormobile, its driver the landlord of the Rose and Crown public house at Bockington, returning from delivering to his home an inebriated customer, found, as he descended the steep hill into the village, that his brakes had failed. Unable therefore to take the bend in the hill at twice his normal speed, his vehicle left the road and plunged down into a copse. Mrs Baxter reported him missing at midnight. By two o'clock he was found by the police and extricated from the vehicle by ambulance men to be rushed to hospital, his condition hovering between life and death.

The following evening Johnny left supper in a mood of some trepidation. (Steve was not with him but eating chez Nick.) He considered the yobbo battle that Nick had arranged a very risky idea. And his reservations were intensified when he made his customary after-supper call on Nick's rooms, for the preparations for a siege that were going on there alarmed his cautious nature. Nick in his role of commander-in-chief was surveying his men and his armoury and giving directions: 'OK everyone, estimated hour of attack: 8.45 p.m., the end of prep. Steve will get behind the hedge on the other side of the path – where are you Steve?'

' 'ere, sir,' replied the commanding officer's number one, the proud bearer of the aforesaid shotgun. 'And you lot' – he turned on his fellows – 'just remember that sir's great-grandfather was at the Battle of Waterloo. We won that one, we're gonna win this one. Right?' He nursed the twelve-bore dotingly, the cartridge belt slung over one shoulder and across his chest, bandit-style.

Other members of the group had armed themselves with various weapons, including air-pistols. A large quantity of small green apples, presumably collected from the tree in the Horse's private garden, constituted the missiles for the catapults. There was an air of pugnacious expectancy in the group, an air fostered by the drinking of bottles of beer.

'Supposing they come along during prep?' suggested Johnny by way of demur.

'Don't fuss, Johnny,' said Nick, naturally anxious to sustain his role as confident strategist and leader before his men. 'Not going, are you? Stay and have a drink. Anyway you haven't seen our secret weapon.'

'No, thanks,' said Johnny. 'I've got some work to do. I'll... I'll be back at the end of prep.' And he hurried away.

As he headed for his own study he contemplated writing an anonymous note to the Horse and putting it under his door. Even the Horse would be obliged to do something about it. And it might be possible for most of the blame to fall upon the Borstal lads rather than upon Nick who seemed to Johnny more deeply committed to the operation than was prudent. By the time he reached his study door, in fact, he was firmly decided on that course of action. This thing just could not go ahead. Of course it would in a sense be a dreadful act of disloyalty on his part – 'sneaking', in small boys' parlance – Nick was expecting his support and he had said he would join him, but he simply couldn't do that, it would be suicide, so even if it meant Nick was furious with him he would have to act. He would... he opened the door: there in his chair, slumped, distraught, weeping: 'Jane!'

❋ CHAPTER 19 ❋

Worse Trouble

'Jane, what the hell... ! – ' but she forestalled any further words by flinging herself into his arms with renewed sobs. Bemused by a combination of surprise and compassion for his beloved, Johnny nonetheless had the presence of mind to back up against the door to prevent anyone else coming into the room. (Locks were forbidden.) 'Jane, whatever's the matter?'

Weeping, she gave him the dreadful news of her father's accident and his condition – still unconscious, still between life and death. By the time she'd finished, the post-supper clamour in the study corridor had died away, the prep bell had gone and working quiet reigned. 'Oh no, oh no... ' Johnny, having now wedged the door closed, knelt at her feet, holding her hands as she told her story. He had to interrupt her account of 'police' and 'identifying the driver' and 'desperately upset' to implore her to whisper but he held her hands all the more lovingly as he did so.

Eventually Jane calmed a bit, the story and most of its details were done, and she said, 'I'm sorry about coming here like this, Johnny – I just had to see you – Mum's out, you know, with him practically all the time and I couldn't bear to be alone.'

'That's all right, that's all right,' Johnny whispered reassuringly. 'Sit down.' Kneeling beside her, he took her in his arms again. 'I'm so sorry,' he said. 'So sorry,' and, 'I love you.'

She sobbed on him and he wiped her wet cheeks with his loving fingers. But what to do next? His intention to write the warning note to the Horse had been completely ousted by the sudden appearance of Jane – it was too late to do anything about it now, and anyway dealing with this situation was naturally uppermost in his mind. Somehow he had to get her out of school and unseen. But at any moment – supposing the yobs arrived in the middle of prep rather than at the end, as planned? – the peace of that hour was going to be shattered by uncouth shouts, flying apples, running, possibly wrestling and punching and, probably, a shotgun blast or two. The whole place would be in turmoil.

In films the hero, faced with a similar act of adventurous stealth to perform as Johnny now had in getting Jane unseen off the premises, would welcome – indeed possibly himself create – a diversion of just that kind. But was it such a good idea? Certainly all authority figures would be alerted by the coming rumpus and turn out to see what was going on, which meant that he would more than likely bump into one of them as he sneaked Jane out. Caught like that, he would be liable on the two charges of being a party to the conflict and having a girl in the school. That would mean more than just a gating – much more. Perhaps then it would be better if they went out together now before everything did happen, while all was yet quiet, there was little on the move and everyone had their heads down. But then members of staff were liable to be walking about at such times and of course any pupil movement would attract all the more attention – let alone pupil-and-girl movement. Perhaps he should send Jane out on her own but clearly she was in no state to concentrate on evasive tactics and would be at a loss to explain herself if challenged over her presence in the school.

'Oh Christ!' he wailed. Nearly an hour of prep was gone. The yobbo invasion was imminent. Both panic and prudence suggested prompt action. He must get her off school premises as soon as possible, not of course by the way she had arrived, which was simply walking across quad as she now still tearfully and to Johnny's horror informed him, but down the back path itself, the shortest and most direct route out. Coaxing her into a sense of urgency combined with caution, Johnny climbed out of his study window and helped her out on to the house lawn. From there to the path was a short distance and this they covered at a loping crouch which was designed to reconcile stealth with speed but must have made them look highly suspicious if observed from one of the many windows – including those of the Horse's own quarters – that overlooked that part of the grounds. Having got to the path, the two, hand in hand, ran like Keats' Porphyro and Madeleine into the storm. Johnny was already hopeful of getting off school premises safely when at a bend in the path they saw others approaching.

'Oh my God, it's the yobbos,' exclaimed Johnny breathlessly and yanked the uncomprehending Jane through a gap in the hedge that bordered the path on the side furthest from the school. Loud, raucous voices approached. Had he and Jane been seen diving out of view? If so, God help them! If not, they had a good hope that the yobs would not notice them behind the thick hedge as they passed by on their way to the battle-ground. He then realised that he and Jane had got no further down the path than a point level with Nick's rooms and that they were therefore going to be, if not in the thick of it, at least on the fringes of the fray and might therefore not escape without being seen or indeed hurt.

' 'ello, Squire,' came then a hoarse whisper nearby and Johnny turned round to see Steve, into whose hiding place they had unknowingly escaped. He was prone on the grass and supporting the beloved shotgun like a marksman with a rifle, its barrels thrust into the hedge, looking ready for action. 'Geddown!' he hissed, flapping a huge hand. The voices were now quieter but they were approaching. Johnny and Jane ducked down on to the grass, still holding hands.

The marauding youths paused just beside them, taking advantage of some shrubbery on the school side of the path to group their forces and gather stones from the path itself. Little did they know that they were within inches of a twelve-bore muzzle and Johnny was in agonies lest Steve be unable to resist the temptation to effect maximum surprise and take them off at the ankles with both barrels. Fortunately the invaders delayed no longer but sprang into action with warlike cries. Not much of this could be seen from behind the hedge in any detail, though Johnny did glimpse one of the attackers take aim with an air pistol and fire it with some effect as the audible tinkling of glass in the direction of the school buildings testified.

Soon the battle heated up and answering warlike shouts could be heard coming from the school side. These were accompanied by several of the missiles that Johnny had earlier that evening seen lined up in readiness and it was not long before their own innocent hiding place began to receive fire as unseen air-gun pellets pinged into the hedge and the occasional little green apple lodged in its greenery.

'Johnny, what's going on?' implored poor Jane, now bewildered and frightened as well as distressed.

'Bit of a fight,' Johnny stated, inadequately. 'Just keep down.'

It was then that Steve rose to his feet and with all the advantage of having his enemy with its back to him sprang into the gap in the hedge and, holding the gun at the hip, let fly with both barrels in the direction of the *mêlée*. The appallingly loud explosions were not followed, to Johnny's relief, by cries of pain but shouts of rage and an intensification in the bombardment, for the lovers' position was now the target of both sides, Steve having sprung back from the gap and behind the hedge again, yelling, 'Come and get me, fuckers!'

Luckily for Johnny and Jane, he now ran alongside the hedge in the direction from which the two of them had originally come. Both spent cartridges having been automatically ejected, Steve had reloaded from his bandolier and was now twenty yards away, presumably with a view to crossing the path further up and outflanking the enemy. This left the two innocents still the object of fire, but mercifully not for long, for Steve loosed off a fresh double discharge, this time into the thick overhanging branches of a pine tree which cascaded twigs, cones and needles down upon the heads of the assailing party.

The battle had moved on. It was time to escape. The authorities would be on the scene at any second. Clasping Jane's hand, Johnny peered through the gap in the hedge and was about to emerge with her and make a run for it when he was pulled up short by the sight of an astonishing figure. This appeared to be a clown-cannibal, naked as to its top half, hung about with strange-coloured ornaments and a headdress cunningly fashioned out of pyjamas. The torso had been decorated in white signs, suggestive of witchcraft. The figure was gyrating and prancing and emitting bloodcurdling cries. That Billy should have got himself involved in this fracas and in so grotesque a get-up was an oddity that his friend had no leisure to ponder.

Johnny had indeed picked the right moment, for the defenders' small arms fire had been suspended in favour of the double act of Steve with the shotgun and Billy with the cannibal war dance performance, while the attackers seemed to have lowered their weapons and slackened their onslaught in disbelief and terror. He and Jane could therefore hope to get away without fear of injury. But alas! the lull was brief. Urged on by another double blast from Nick's twelve-bore and by the still capering figure of Billy in war paint – presumably the 'secret weapon' to which Nick had earlier referred – the yobbos had taken to their heels and were even now, as Johnny and Jane took to their heels, close upon them, fugitives in flight from fugitives. Down the narrow path they all now fled. And thus it was that the school porter, a man of huge build and wartime experience, well placed at a turn in the path, collected substantial numbers of troublemakers, Johnny being his first prey and concluding with the foremost of the pursuers, Steve and Billy. It was the lot of the master present – none other, of course, than the Burk – to take into his arms the wholly bewildered, breathless and tearful Jane.

❋ CHAPTER 20 ❋

In the
Wilderness

Disciplinary action was instantaneous and condign. The Borstal lads were bundled into their minibus that same night and returned to their home institution where they were much in demand for an account of the evening's events. The central implication of Nick and the lurid part played by Billy resulted in expulsion of them both, 'no shriving time allowed'. In Nick's case the offender's complete lack of commitment to school life was added to the scales, similarly in Billy's, with the addition of the heavy suspicion he was under after the affair of the books on the fire engine, and so the school's equivalent of capital punishment was handed down to both members. The next morning saw the two taking their last taxi down the drive.

It was a sad day for Johnny, that two of his closest friends should be thus summarily cut off. Nick's rooms were sealed up. His intention of demonstrating the total unsuitability of his quarters for girl accommodation owing to their vulnerability to outside interference failed totally and the school workmen soon moved in, under the Burk's complacent and the Horse's uncomplaining eyes, to prepare it for just that purpose.

And as for Johnny, he too could not go unpunished. He asserted his lack of involvement in the episode and Nick had corroborated his assertion so he was cleared on that score. Then as to the offence of having a girl in his study, he was cleared of that too by Jane's tearful explanation to the Burk who had consoled and returned her to her anxious mother at Bockington. Johnny was merely gated – again – a punishment which though it would separate him from his precious Jane was not too serious and could be kept, as before, from his parents' knowledge. This time, however, the gating was total: no school trips, no saint's day exemption, and Johnny realised that to break his gating would be to incur the punishment that had befallen his friends.

And so there fell a bleakness upon his soul the like of which he could not remember. Two of his closest companions had suddenly vanished from his life, as if by death. What had come over them that they had acted in such a rash way, Johnny wondered? It seemed like suicide.

'More like boredom, really, I suppose,' opined Angus with whom Johnny was wandering on the Downs a few days later. 'A feeling of imprisonment.'

'Well, we all get that,' said Johnny, thinking of Jane and his enforced separation from her.

'Sure, but some people fret more than others.'

'What'll they be doing now, d'you think?'

'Nick'll be at the races and the club, he'll get a high-paid job through an uncle in some big city company – in three months he won't remember our names.'

'And Billy?'

'Probably gone back to run his country. In a few years' time he'll be its president. But we're not like that, are we?' said Angus.

'No,' agreed Johnny, 'we're just ordinary and boring, doing our A Levels, playing cricket, trying to be good.'

'It's a bit better than that,' said Angus. 'We've got girls: my Angela, your Jane.'

'Well, sort of,' agreed Johnny.

Ah Jane! At mention of her name Johnny's heart – or was it

his stomach, or perhaps both? – rose and sank in sickening simultaneity. How he loved her! How he wished to be with her, to talk to and comfort her, to get news of her father! Angus recommended ringing her but Johnny was not comfortable with the telephone, he couldn't bear the terrible immediacy-with-distance of it. But neither could he find the right words in his letters to her. He had written straightaway to give her the bad news of his gating and to tell her that she mustn't under any circumstances come to see him at Worthington. Otherwise what could he say? When she had been in his study and in his arms he hadn't known the right words then either, but that hadn't mattered – she hadn't wanted words, she'd wanted him. Perhaps all she still wanted was him but he couldn't send himself by post – words were all he had and what could he say? 'I expect you're feeling desperately upset about your father's condition… I can't imagine what it must be like… How is your mother taking it… what will she/you do if… ' And he hadn't heard from her to give him a clue, to give him anything to go on. Perhaps that kind of shock and grief just blew adolescent love to pieces. Oh Jane!

But he did write to her, haltingly, simply, sending love, telling her what happened after the fateful evening, feeding her little snippets of school news, such as they were. It was all sad and dreary and he sank into one of those periods of sloth that are so easily entered into in boarding school and so hard to climb out of when there was no change of scene. It was as if the world of adulthood – that heady world of pubs and films and girlfriends – so briefly tasted was suddenly dashed from his lips to be replaced by nothing better than school routine: work, cricket, a walk and smoke with a friend – the old simplicities.

Johnny had managed little more than two weeks and barely three hopelessly inadequate letters to Jane when he received – at last – something from her. He had desperately missed her letters but had tried to tell himself that he couldn't expect them in the circumstances. Nonetheless he had hoped, knowing in his heart that their separation was hurting her as much as him, feeling deep down sure that she would want to write, that she would find the time to write, however she might be feeling about her father's condition. What arrived more than vindicated his faith. It was not the usual, ordinary envelope – it felt more like a magazine. Indeed, when Johnny got it to his study and tore it open with nervous fingers it turned out to be an exercise book – one of the cheap, flimsy ones to be had at Woolworth's – and it was entirely filled with her writing. Good God! thought Johnny, was she writing a novel or something? But no, it was a letter all right. He looked at the beginning – 'My Dearest Johnny... ' and flipped to the end: 'So Much Love, Jane'. The entire bloody thing was a single letter! Incredible! Or rather it was a sort of diary-letter because it was broken into sections, each headed with a date.

'My Dearest Johnny,' he read, and those words ran like balm over his soul, 'I don't know what to say but you know me I'll say it anyway and I must talk to you – well, it does feel like talking – I just don't know where I am. Sometimes when I think if Dad should die I feel almost as if he's died already and I'm just getting used to it. I visit him often, nearly every day – Mum is there half the time – and I feel I could bear it so much better if you were with me though it's not a nice sight Dad lying there as if he were dead. Oh, I know I'm drivelling on but what else can I do? I keep hoping you'll ring and then when the phone goes I do hope it's not you because I know that if it is all I'll do is cry and what'll be the good of that? Please write to me. Tell me what happened after that awful evening at school. Tell me how you are, what you're doing. If you can't think of things to say just write 'My Dearest Jane, Your ever-loving Johnny.'

'June 14th: Now the doctors say that there is some hope that Dad will survive and I'm so happy I don't know what to say.' But actually she did because she wrote another side or so for the day and Johnny was in tears to read it as she was in tears to write it. The exercise book chronicled her feelings and thoughts for the two-week period following the accident. As she admitted herself, it was less of a letter and more of a tearful ramble, and she begged his forgiveness several times for burdening him with it all – as if he would have wished to escape such a burden: didn't she understand?

'June 16th: The incredible thing is that just because someone you love is on the point of death it doesn't mean that ordinary everyday life stops. You still go on walking and eating meals (sort of) and watching the milkman making his delivery – I suppose you have to really unless you're going to give up hope too which isn't right either but it seems an insult to the person lying there somehow to carry on living. I suppose Mum was right when she said, 'We must try and carry on as normal' and so I've been going to school every day, even though my exams are all over now, just the same for Dad's being where he is and she's working hard to keep the pub going – it's our living, she explains, we have to stay open, and I help too every evening and at weekends and other friends and neighbours come in, everyone's being fantastically kind – and that makes you want to cry too!!! But how I wish you could be with us as well, you're such a help and it would help us both to bear it all. Of course, as Mum says, we'll have to think about our longer-term future in case the worst happens and even if he lives he can't be – well, exactly as he was, but I say Not yet, I don't want to think about it. Supposing we have to go to some other part of the country, I couldn't bear it.'

And here the inexorable bells of school life warned Johnny to be off to somewhere or other so to somewhere or other he duly went, the precious letter-diary secreted in his study for his return. He decided he would not eat it all in one go anyway – it was going to have to last, perhaps for a week or more; he would eke it out and savour it. So he had read little past June 16th – instead going back and relishing earlier bits – by the time of his next tutorial with the Burk. This was never a welcome event but it was now all the more unwelcome on account of Jane's recent encounter with him and his involvement with her over the Nick and the yobbos affair.

The Burk, of course, had been immensely pleased by his successful part in netting the miscreants in that regrettable episode and assisting their expulsion from the school. He would undoubtedly want to talk about it and to discuss Jane with him. Johnny's heart was heavy as he made his way up the great wooden staircase of the Founder's Tower. And his heart sank further when the tray laid for tea beside the open window indicated that another session on the leads was in view. The Burk, perhaps sensing his victim's disadvantage, was in brisk form. Having duly taken up position in the sunshine on the leaded roof, they talked of cricket – Johnny's house had somehow luckily made it through the first round of the house matches – and of his Maths O Level retake at which he blushed because it made him think of Jane.

A silence followed and a certain deepening of the atmosphere: the inevitable topic was upon them. Johnny's gaze wandered northward over the roofs of the school buildings and in the direction of Bockington. Oh to be there!

'I'm glad,' began the Burk portentously, 'that your involvement in the violent events of the other evening was not any deeper. Your career at school might have suffered the same premature termination as… ' – he couldn't bring himself to name his two enemies – 'your friends. I am glad for your sake, I must say, that they are gone since I don't think they were the best influence on you.'

'No, sir,' replied Johnny, hoping that simple agreement would hurry him away from the topic. He knew the bastard was at least partly right but he didn't wish to hear it.

'There are, however, other ways of blighting a school career… Perhaps you know what I am referring to,' the Burk continued in measured but sympathetically halting terms. 'I spoke to your… friend, Jane Baxter – whom as you probably know I have met in connection with the possibility of her becoming one of the pioneering group of girls to enter the school in September – I spoke to her after the incident and have spoken to her since. She is a… I cannot disapprove of the relationship in itself but I think it better that she be allowed to concentrate on overcoming the difficulty she faces at home, I mean of course her... father... and I think you too would do well to concentrate on your work for the remaining weeks of term.'

Hearing Jane actually named and discussed by the appalling Burk was a new horror but Johnny noted that the man did seem to experience some genuine difficulty in expressing himself. Though he was ponderous and self-important as usual it was almost as if he had some idea of the sensitivity of the subject. Had Jane made to the Burk a confession of her love? And why should the Burk have spoken to her 'since' the incident? Johnny didn't like to ask and only managed a falteringly acquiescent, 'Yes, sir, I'll... ' by way of reply. This appeared to satisfy the Burk who pursued the subject no further, but it drove Johnny back to Jane's letter with the additional curiosity as to what, if anything, she had to say about the Burk.

❊ CHAPTER 21 ❊

Back
on Track

June 17th was informative. Jane related how Mr Burkinshaw had taken her to his room after the yobbo episode, how he had been very kind and understanding to her and telephoned her mother to let her know what had happened, and how he had driven her home.

'I know you and your friends scorn Mr Burkinshaw but actually I think he is quite nice – he is always very friendly and polite to me, though Mummy doesn't seem to have taken to him. I know he's not very good-looking but that doesn't matter.' And actually Johnny, when he thought about it, had to admit that the Burk was not looking quite as repulsive as he once had. Perhaps it was the fine weather and fresh air. His bald head, normally white and flaky, you might have expected to go red instead under the effect of sunshine but in fact it had tanned and he had a rather more presentable appearance. Perhaps it was being in love! – though it was unimaginable that the feeling he had for Miss Whatshername at St Agnes could in any way match the feeling he had for Jane. Perhaps it was that in order to front 'the girl operation' he had to spruce himself up a bit for the benefit of the mums.

A day or two further on in the diary and Jane was still in distress over her father and filling pages and pages of rapid writing with not a lot of punctuation. 'It's a bit depressing', she wrote, 'about the future, I didn't want to talk about it at first and Mummy agreed but then I thought we must think about it because how can we get settled in our minds if we don't know what's to become of us? Well, and this was not long after Mr B. visited us which was kind of him though he didn't stay long and Mummy wasn't very welcoming, as I mentioned before she doesn't seem to like him at all, it's not very good news for us I'm afraid because one thing is now definite she says, and that is I'm not coming to Worthington in September. As I said before Mum never seemed very keen about it and now Dad's the way he is we can't possibly afford it. The money we get for the pub which we might well have to sell we will need in order to buy an ordinary house. Of course I'm so disappointed. Oh, when am I going to see you? I do so long to talk to you. Thank you so so so much for your letter which I loved, and I'm so sorry about Nick and Billy, please write again, soon, don't worry about what to say or being careful not to upset me about Dad – just WRITE !!! I think I'd better stop here, apart from anything else I'm practically at the end of the book.'

There was now barely a fortnight to the end of term, which was good, of course, for the usual reasons and good because it meant the freedom to see Jane again, but not so good with thirty miles between their homes and Jane perhaps to move to some other part of the country. Before, she was either going to be at Worthington, with all the pluses and minuses that entailed, or she would be at home in Bockington; either way they were going to be able to carry on their relationship. But after what had happened to her Dad everything was different and uncertain. The only positive thing that now occupied any of Johnny's heart and mind was cricket. His house, under Angus' captaincy, having got through the first round of the house competition, suddenly began to believe in itself and Angus, with Johnny's help, often had the team in the nets of an evening after prep practising for the next encounter. On the very edge of the school grounds and close to the northern boundary, the nets seemed a taunting reminder to Johnny of times he had left the school by that route, headed for Halfway House. Would that rendezvous ever see them again? Would they ever be lying on the grass together, hand-in-hand, looking up at the sky and talking, talking?

'Well, think we can beat them?' asked Johnny as he and Angus sauntered along to the ground for the semifinal.

'We beat the first lot,' was his friend's reply.

'True, though they didn't have first eleven bowlers. Now what you need is Angela on the boundary,' teased Johnny, 'to give you spirit.'

'What – like you had Jane at Clouds?'

'Ha ha.'

In truth they neither of them really thought they could win this contest in spite of their former sporting success. Nor, having won the toss, did their team's performance with the bat give grounds for any great hopes. In no time they were three wickets down for a paltry forty-odd with Angus still in and Johnny, the last recognised batsman, yet to come. Waiting nervously in the pavilion for the next inevitable wicket to fall, Johnny reflected how lucky the house had been to get even so far as to meet the probable winners in the semifinal. And, going in to bat, when the next wicket had indeed fallen in the following over and the Horse had wished him good luck on his way out, Johnny's outlook was even less sanguine. Angus, greeting him in the mid-field, was attempting to hang on to the innings in spite of the sixty-for-five on the board.

'OK,' he said. 'Look for runs – we've got to keep the score on the move – but don't take any risks.'

Johnny nodded. He suddenly felt curiously relaxed. No great things were expected of him and if he went down promptly, well, the house wasn't going to win anyway. With this attitude he proceeded to bat with a mature calm that enabled him to keep his eye on the ball and indeed take no risks. Consequently, with Angus at the other end, his eye now well in and the opposition's powerful opening bowlers starting to tire, the partnership began to blossom and runs began to flow. It was in fact when they were on ninety-nine and on the verge of putting the game in a different perspective that something quite unpredictable happened to jeopardise the partnership.

Batsmen, during most of their time at the wicket spent in not addressing themselves to the ball, tend to stroll about with an air, real or assumed, of ease. They prod the odd divot, perhaps exchange a brief word with the umpire, they glance at the scoreboard, leaning on the trusty willow, and scan the unpeopled boundary. It was while engaged in this last activity, as the bowling changed ends, that Johnny's attention became suddenly riveted upon a sight that had absolutely nothing to do with the crucial business in hand and that represented a very serious threat to his concentration. For what had appeared on the boundary was a person whose distinctly familiar bearing – though it was too far to distinguish features – declared herself to be none other than Jane.

Surprise, excitement, apprehension, all sprang to life in him and instantly his cricketing concentration was in danger. There was also an ominous feeling of *déjà-vu*, that time Angus had referred to just before the game when Jane had turned up unexpectedly on the boundary at Clouds. It did not bode well. But there she was – here and now – his Jane, whom he hadn't seen since that fateful evening of the news of her father's accident; his Jane, whose exercise-book-long letter-diary was his most treasured possession – she who now, all alone, strolled the boundary, aware of him. A deep and sweeping pathos collected about that solitary figure in Johnny's mind as he looked at her. How he longed to dash over and take her in his arms!

'Yes!'

Christ they were running! Angus had struck the ball into the covers somewhere and they were pelting down the wicket. Johnny made his ground comfortably but he had been caught more than a little off-guard and addressed himself now to the crease at the further end of the wicket from Jane's boundary in a distinctly flustered state. Not that he went completely to pieces as a result of this flurry but the need to concentrate on the game and the terrific magnetic pull of his beloved waged fearful battle within him. He tried hard to give the proceedings on the field his full attention when it was crucial to do so, but when he had a moment off – between balls when not facing, say – he allowed his gaze to shoot out and fasten on the beloved figure. Obviously he couldn't wave or anything so he just stared as hard and as long as he could and hoped she could tell. At one stage she made a sort of gesture that might have been intended as a discreet wave and he part-responded with a small lift of his gloved hand, though his arm remained at his side. Would she notice?

Having turned things over in his mind and having achieved an unusually long span of cricketing concentration in which he had actually scored more runs and with Angus taken the total up to a hundred-and-twenty, he now rewarded himself with another glance in her direction. She had gone. Desperately Johnny scanned the entire boundary but she was nowhere to be seen. Between balls he looked searchingly in all directions – up towards the school, down the first stretch of the drive, by the pavilion. Nothing. Oh God! – not another disappearing act by Jane at the cricket field! At least this time – unlike at Clouds – he wasn't in a state of sin, as it were, he hadn't been disloyal to her, so she couldn't have walked off in disgust. On the contrary, he was doing rather well, he thought, hoping that Jane could make out on the board his steadily mounting total of runs. Perhaps she had realised, after all that had happened, that she mustn't be seen with him again: surely she wasn't supposed to be at the school and certainly it would not go down well with the authorities if they were seen together. But then if so, how cruel of her just to turn up, wave and go away again.

If Jane's sudden appearance had disconcerted him her equally sudden disappearance disconcerted him more. Desperate with frustration at having had her so near and now having lost her, Johnny soon lost his wicket also, playing a shot without due concentration. His trudge back to the pavilion was therefore doubly gloomy, a gloom in no way lifted by the Horse's hearty, 'Well done, Clarke'. Then alone in the changing room and beginning to feel more and more sorry for himself – why could things not go smoothly? why did things have to keep going wrong? – he heard behind him the same words but in a very different voice.

'Well done.'

'Christ, Jane – what are *you* doing here! I mean – what are you *doing* here?' He left the room and edged her into a little corridor where they could talk perhaps unnoticed. 'You don't half have a habit of turning up out of the blue!'

'I thought you'd be glad to see me – I'm glad to see *you*.'

'Of course I am, I am, but – you rather put me off my batting, you know.'

'I thought it might give you encouragement. I'm sorry,' said Jane and she looked it and so Johnny felt upset because he hadn't wanted to say what he had.

'No, I'm sorry,' he said. 'It's just a bit of a shock and I don't think we should be seen together. But I am so pleased to see you.' He wanted to take her in his arms and hug her and kiss her. 'We'll meet at the nets. You go on down, on your own. I'll come in a minute. I don't know how long we'll have – doesn't look as if our innings is going to last much longer. See you in a minute.'

Safely out of sight from the pavilion and a good distance from anyone, they could hold hands.

'Thanks for your letter,' said Johnny.

'Call it a letter – I was just letting off my feelings. I shouldn't have thrown all that lot at you.'

'I loved every word. Now, so what's going on? You just decided to turn up? Did you know I'd be playing cricket?'

'No. I've been here on official business.'

'What do you mean – 'official business'?'

'Interviews, tests – for the girls' scholarships.'

'But I thought you weren't coming – because of the money.'

'Well, that's what the scholarship's for – to win the money so that I can come.'

Johnny was lost. 'But a scholarship doesn't usually pay for everything.'

'I know, but apparently all that's been sorted out – I don't know why, I don't really understand it. Perhaps because I'm sort of half an orphan now. Mum seems quite strange about it, I suppose it's the worry and the fear, making her odd. Oh, Johnny, it is wonderful to see you again. I've missed you so much.'

'I've missed you too.'

Oh how soft she was and sad and needing him! But anything more than holding hands was not on while they were on school premises, even out of sight as now.

'So the Burk's been interviewing you again, has he? I think he's got a crush on you, you know.' The idea made him feel slightly sick.

'He's being ever so helpful. Oh, I do hope it's going to work out, Johnny.'

'But when are we going to meet? This is no good and it's risky and I absolutely cannot leave school. We'll have to wait till the end of term. When will you know about your scholarship?'

'They say before the end of term.'

'Oh, God – write to me – write to me every day.'

'Twice a day I'll write.'

'Three times – all the time! Jane, you must go – and I must go too, Angus can't be holding out this long – we'll be fielding any minute.'

'Kiss me goodbye,' she said, smiling up at him.

To hell with the risk – he kissed her.

✱ CHAPTER 22 ✱

A Revelation

S peech Day was not the only occasion in the Worthington summer term calendar to send shivers of horror down the spine of any true wag. There was also Old Boys' Day.

On this occasion former pupils of varying generations would return to the school and mooch about. Certain entertainments would be laid on, such as a chapel service, at which many a knee long unused to bend would adopt an attitude of forgotten reverence. The CCF band would play nostalgic tunes to nostalgic ears and the Headmaster would give an address in which the school's successes and developments since 'your day' was spiced by anecdotes provided him by senior members of Common Room. On this occasion, of course, he made much of the introduction of girls, not without jocose man-of-the-world reference to the living-in serving girls of the 1930s who, according to legend, had provided the bloods of that era with a form of education not included in the prospectus. There was also cricket to watch, of which more later.

Old Boys came in three broad categories. There was the most senior, their old boys' ties faded and frayed, who stomped about the place attempting to locate their names on boards fastened high up on walls of dingy corridors – The Cricket XI 1912 – and their eyes quietly alight with the memory of juvenile misdemeanour and punishment. Then there were the middle-aged. These had mostly an apologetic manner, their ties the only things bold about them, for those who were successful in life rarely bothered to attend such backward-looking occasions. Even if accompanied by their (usually dowdy) wives, they seemed as solitary on this day as during their time at the school, and presented a questing air, as if wondering whether 'the splendour in the grass' that they had somehow missed at the time might in some way, even now, be discoverable. The third category comprised the juniors, ties brilliant and fresh in their concatenation of colour, their pockets jangling with money, car keys dangling ostentatiously from the belt of slightly too casual clothes, cigarettes and matches permanently in one hand, self-conscious girlfriend in the other; these still celebrated their membership of the beloved community from which they did not yet realise they were separated for ever.

Wags generally made an early departure on this day to Bishopstown, returning only in the late evening when all old boys but the few who enjoyed a whisky-drinking relationship with their former housemasters would have departed. Unfortunately, the customary old boys' cricket match could not, through a failure of organisation, be played this year, and the school authorities, knowing how important a game of cricket was to the whole occasion, had decreed that the final of the house matches should be played instead. Perhaps they hoped that a certain residual house spirit might be kindled in the breasts of those old boys lucky enough to have belonged to one of the contesting houses. This game – for their house had been miraculously and against the odds victors in the semi-final – condemned Angus and Johnny to remaining at school the entire day.

The old boys being, as a class, of no interest to him, Johnny paid them little attention. What therefore was his delight and astonishment when, as he was preparing himself for the house final, who should burst unceremoniously into his study but Nick and Billy?

'Good God!'

'Yes, we thought you might be surprised to see two of Worthington's most noble sons.'

'But you're not exactly old boys.'

'Well, we're certainly not present pupils – ergo we must be old boys,' Nick argued.

He looked to Johnny very strange, dressed as he was in a rather elegant light-weight grey suit. Needless to say, he sported none of the appurtenances of manhood like car keys and cigarettes previously referred to as the required equipment of the young old boy and of course neither he nor Billy was wearing the old boys' tie.

'Though indeed,' continued Nick, 'we do not qualify for membership and have not actually been invited to this festal day. However, we wished to see you and considered that nobody could bodily remove us from the premises – it would be far too embarrassing for them.'

In something of a contrast to Nick's suave appearance, Billy presented a striking picture, being dressed from head to foot in black, suede and leather featuring prominently in the material of his get-up. From his fedora to his chukka boots no colour or white was to be seen – he had even concealed the whites of his eyes with dark glasses. There was only one thing that deviated from this monochromatic appearance and that was the badge he wore on his shirt. This, though with a black background, featured a sort of inverted trident in white, and indicated, Johnny knew, commitment to a campaign for the abandonment of nuclear weaponry.

'Well, this is a surprise – didn't expect to see you,' Johnny found himself saying somewhat uninvitingly. He felt strange in the company of his old friends now so far removed from him in many ways.

'We have come to admire the old place,' Nick replied with airy facetiousness, 'relive old memories – that sort of thing.'

'Like hell.'

'Quite.'

They made their way down to the cricket field, Billy sloping off on some undeclared purpose of his own. Nick greeted staff with patronising civility and ignored all the boys, many of whom stared at him and nudged one another. The embarrassment he ought by rights to have felt he somehow contrived to transfer on to other people and the Creep unconvincingly pretended not to see him.

'Still going out with Jane?' Nick enquired as they walked.

'When you're gated going out isn't exactly on,' Johnny returned glumly. 'But yes, we are still writing and… so on.'

'And is she to be joining the first intake of girls in September?'

'Yes – it's been a bit up and down, that one, but she's taken a scholarship.'

'Up and down?' Nick queried.

'Well, on and off. As a matter of fact she's coming here this evening. She's got to see the Burk again about things – she's always seeing the Burk. Then we're going to risk a long walk up to the Ring. Thanks for asking.'

Nick looked unusually reflective. Nearing the Pavilion and the people gathered there for the game, he said, 'I think I'll steer away from that lot. Join me on the bank when you're done. Looks as if you're batting.'

Angus returning from the wicket for the toss was making the gesture signifying as much and Johnny went off to pad up. There was no doubt he felt awkward about Nick and Billy's visit. School and these two simply didn't go together any more even if they were still his friends. Besides, he reflected a little guiltily, what would the authorities think seeing him with them? And why exactly had they come today?

At the crease Johnny again found concentration difficult. At least Jane wasn't hovering on the boundary to put him off, though she might well turn up later. What would be the outcome this time of her official visit? The feebleness of his concentration soon took its toll and it was as early as the second over of their innings that a good ball just outside the off-stump had him groping ineptly, he got the outside edge the bowler was looking for and the ball sailed with infuriating inevitability into second slip's hands. He returned to Nick on the remote bank boundary – the outfield had for some of its length been cut into the slope of the hill – on which his friend sprawled, smoking.

'Bloody stupid,' he grumbled, annoyed with himself.

'I never had a very good influence on you, did I?' said Nick. 'But Johnny, I could have put you off a hell of a lot more if I'd told you something I know.'

'Something you know?'

'Yes, and something I'd better tell you now.'

Johnny's blood ran cold. (The hackneyed phrase is not wrong.) Christ! What was coming now? Nick had terminal cancer? He, Johnny, was boring, thick and unattractive? What horror could he have in store?

'What's it about?' he asked.

'You remember how I encountered at the club earlier this term an aged sod who appeared quite by chance to have the goods on the Burk?'

'The Burk? Oh, yes – something to do with… – what was it?'

'An unspecified indiscretion – probably of a sexual nature – that was not at the time further defined. But since then… '

'Hey, you haven't picked up the whole story, have you?' Johnny enquired, his own initial anxiety as to the nature of Nick's portentous announcement now having faded and his glee gathering fast; this could be a feast for him to share in the Waggery later. 'Tell, tell!'

'I have again encountered the aged bugger – an ancient mariner, in fact, as it turns out, an admiral – who originally divulged the first tantalising bits of information.'

'Well, go on.'

'Don't hurry me. The whole thing is rather like a Victorian novel – it takes time to tell as well as having an indiscretion at its heart. Now, while a bachelor gay at his previous establishment up in the north, the Burk got into a relationship with a local girl. No doubt he was driven to a frenzy of lust by the suppression of all his natural instincts. She was employed in the village pub – a simple girl… ' Nick paused. He was staring out over the field with a somewhat abstracted air. There was in his narrative now none of the relish appropriate to the telling of a scandalous anecdote. Johnny's glee abated, his initial apprehension seeping back into his soul. If this was just something juicy about the Burk's past why this sombre manner? Why was it something Nick 'had better tell' him? What could it have to do with him? 'The relationship,' Nick resumed, 'became physical and the consequence was… ' Nick paused, 'natural.'

'The Burk made the barmaid pregnant?'

'That's right.'

'And that's why he was sort of sacked? Well, that explains it.' Johnny was now remembering that first talk with the Burk up on the roof when the horrible man had got rather intense and confidential about innocence and ignorance being a dangerous thing in a young person when it came to the matter of sex – though of course he hadn't used that word – and Johnny had wondered what the Burk's pedagogic platitudes were based on. 'Now that I come to think of it, it makes sense. Well, well, that's pretty juicy. But – hang on. How do you know all this?'

'The ancient mariner, I told you. After our first encounter and hearing what I said about the Burk being at Worthington he took it upon himself to do some research.'

'I see. So what are you intending to do about it? Spot of blackmail?'

Nick didn't smile. 'I'm keeping it in reserve for the time being,' he said. 'It depends what happens.'

'What happens? How do you mean?'

'Well, you'll remember I said I needed to tell you.'

'Yes, why exactly?'

At this point Billy reappeared. He now held a handful of books and he didn't look quite his collected self. 'So much for that bastard,' he said, slumping down on the bank beside them. 'I got my books back.'

'Your books? What books?'

'The ones I left on the fire engine – don't you remember?'

'Oh – those. Yes. You mean you calmly went up to the Burk and demanded them?'

'He wasn't there. I went in, took them. Left a note.'

'Saying?'

' 'My books, you old fornicator.' '

' 'fornicator'? You were being polite – why not 'fucker'?' queried Johnny, amused.

'Hasn't Nick told you?'

'Hang on, Billy,' Nick interposed quickly. 'No, I haven't told Johnny the full story yet. By the way, Johnny, did I mention we had lunch at Bockington on the way here.'

'Christ, did you? Did you see Jane?'

'Yes, but not to talk to – she was doing her duty serving food. I had a conversation with her mother, though.'

'She's nice, isn't she?'

'Yes. A woman of no pretension – touch of a Yorkshire accent – very homely. She was very interested in Worthington.'

'Ummm, she would be. I expect you gave her your view of the Burk.'

'She was very interested in that too. You see, Johnny... '

But again the revelation was prevented. Stern and angry voices were heard from the top of the bank above them.

'You have no right to be at the College!' It was the Creep, accompanied by the Burk and the school porter in uniform.

'There is a taxi here,' added the Burk with what he took to be magisterial iciness of an unanswerable timbre. 'Get into it and leave the school at once. Do not come back.'

'At once,' replied Nick after only a moment's pause and getting to his feet in a leisurely manner. 'I think our business is done – and of course if you've laid on transport for us, who are we to refuse? I trust the driver is already paid.'

Above their heads the three dark figures stood, waiting. Nick brushed a blade or two of grass from his suit trousers with studied nonchalance. 'Ah, no – my business is not quite complete. I was saying, Johnny... ' – and here he raised his voice so that the three lowering figures could not choose but hear – 'I was telling you of a certain person's indiscretion. The barmaid with whom he rashly coupled having become pregnant moved with her shame to the south of the country and soon married a man who ran the public house in which she went to work. Her shame was thus concealed in respectable marriage and the issue of the indiscretion was born legitimately.' He spoke for effect, choosing his words and raising his voice as if on stage. 'You must believe me when I tell you with great regret but complete truth that the pub to which she went is in a village near here... '

There was a swooping – down the bank upon them rushed the Burk. Breaking the speed of his precipitate descent by grasping Nick's arm, he bore his captive away to the waiting taxi while his two fellows, having similarly swooped on Billy, marched him in the same direction. But before he was off the scene Nick had turned to throw over his shoulder at Johnny the now inevitable and terrible words: '...and it is called the Rose and Crown.'

❊ CHAPTER 23 ❊

Fire! Fire!

Just as the Burk had swooped upon the truth-telling Nick, so now there swooped upon Johnny the dark horror of his position: he was in love with the Burk's illegitimate daughter. It was terrible. Incredible. And yet Johnny somehow knew it was true; he knew by the speed with which his heart sank in dread.

Mercifully his batting was done and he was at relative leisure in the field, on his own with time to reflect. Walking in with the bowler, he absently turned over all the circumstances that supported this appalling fact. For a start there was the personal note in the Burk's words during that conversation on the leads of the Founder's Tower about 'juvenile indiscretion'. Then there was absolutely no reason to question Nick's source of information at the club. Most significantly, perhaps, was Jane's mother's reaction to it all, the on-and-off quality in the likelihood of Jane's coming to the school. And hadn't Jane said something about her mother not taking to the Burk? More than understandable if the story were true! In addition to all that was the amount of time Jane had spent with him. Did that mean he knew too? Surely he must. Meeting her mother again he must know. Oh God!

Somehow, preoccupied as he was, Johnny managed to do his duty in the outfield – he even took a catch – and the opposition's wickets were falling. Next thought: was there any family resemblance? Did Jane look like the Burk? What a horrific concept! Well, no, surely not, no, you wouldn't think of them as in any way alike. Would you? Not that unlikeness proved anything. But there was the matter of her mind. Jane was intelligent and obviously going to do well in her O Levels so had she inherited her father's brain, his academic prowess? It was said, wasn't it? that Jane's mother was a village girl – not highly educated. That didn't mean she was dim, of course, but Jane seemed to have that enthusiasm for learning that characterised the Burk. Oh God! But then against that there was the matter of personality. The Burk was horrible – self-conceited and lacking natural warmth – while Jane was modest and shy and loving: how could she possibly be his daughter? Wasn't she much more like Mr Baxter? And yet not only was the Burk nice to Jane, according to her, but also she liked him – she'd said so more than once. Was this a natural affinity coming out? She found herself liking him for the simple reason that he was her natural father! Oh God, God, God!

That Johnny's house should win the final of the house matches was a miracle somewhat wasted on Johnny himself in the circumstances. They had been total outsiders but they had won it – after fifty years they had won it. The rest of the house – and the Horse – were delirious. Tremendous celebrations were instantly put in hand, principally a camp fire supper to be cooked in the house garden that evening and to be enjoyed by all its members. But that he should get a summons from the Burk immediately the match was over came as no surprise to Johnny.

How should he conduct himself in the interview? What line would the Burk himself take? The man knew what Nick had divulged. He knew of Johnny's relationship with Jane. If the story were true would he admit to it, or seek to deny it? If it were true and the truth was out then he had had it – no girls' housemastering for him, no possible future as a headmaster. So his only hope was to deny it. But if he did, there was Jane's mother to call him a liar any time she chose. Equally, a disaster for the Burk. Then there was the matter of what, if anything, he would be saying to Jane when she came later – but that would have to wait. Johnny trudged up the august wooden stairs and knocked on the august wooden door.

'I thought that as your tutor,' the Burk began as Johnny entered, 'I'd better set your mind at rest following that unpleasant episode earlier this afternoon. Your former friends have excelled themselves in malice, incidentally more than justifying the very serious reservations about them that I formed long ago. One of them, as you realise, has fabricated a scandalous untruth about me and chosen to disseminate it. You will know to give it no credit whatever – as indeed will any other responsible persons hearing of it, particularly when they know of the animosity with which those two boys regarded me. Pure malice, pure vindictiveness.'

Johnny was silent. Part of him wanted to believe the Burk's assertion for if it were true then the horror of Jane's being this revolting man's daughter was eliminated – and wouldn't that be wonderful? The other part of him was not so sure. Had the Burk not indicated in an earlier conversation that to err was human? Had he not hinted that he himself might not be entirely above reproach? If so, where had that hint gone now? Where was the human being inside the schoolmaster? Johnny had been brought up to believe and to trust and to respect adults and he was duly inclined to do so. Thus he could not bring himself to believe that one of his masters could be a liar. But here and now the adult in front of him was a pompous blusterer whom he was disinclined to believe and whom he did not like. If there were 'malice and vindictiveness' in Nick's story-telling then there was just as much in the Burk's tone: how he loathed Nick and Billy! Whom would Johnny trust – his friend or his tutor? Whom should he believe?

'So I am depending on you', the unpleasant voice resumed, 'to suppress any inclination to repeat this slander. And I say that, not for my sake or for the sake of truth, but – and you will appreciate this – for the sake of Jane Baxter, who joins us next term. It would be grossly unfair to the girl if she discovered herself to be the subject of such a baseless rumour. Particularly in the circumstances of her father's dreadful accident.' He paused to give Johnny the opportunity for reply. Again Johnny was silent. 'Don't you agree?' persisted the Burk.

For perhaps the first time in his life the automatic words 'Yes, sir' just wouldn't report for duty in Johnny's mouth. They were instilled from birth in his unconscious as well as his conscious mind, drilled and practised over his childhood so that they could perform their tasks without question or complaint, without seeking for any reward, but now they tripped and fell at his feet, useless, and they would not get up.

'I must press you for a reply, Clarke,' the Burk pursued with growing intensity. 'I must press you for your compliance – for the sake of the girl.'

'I don't know what to say, sir,' Johnny replied weakly. Although 'Yes, sir' had defaulted and deserted at last nothing more bold had yet risen to take its place. 'I don't believe you and you're a complete bastard' were not – though they were the thoughts of his heart – in his power to express.

They were saved from further awkwardness by a light tap at the door. It was Jane. Admitting her, the Burk said for Johnny's benefit, 'Jane has come to discuss her Latin – with a view to some coaching during the holidays.' Jane was momentarily surprised to see Johnny there but otherwise looked composed enough – and oh so pretty! How much did she know or guess or wonder? The innocence shone in her face and Johnny felt suddenly a great gulf between them. The Burk with his vileness and untruthfulness had fouled Johnny's own soul but he had not yet harmed Jane. Johnny hated leaving her with him but it was a chance to escape that he must take. He had held the Burk off for a time but the man would be back – he was not one to let such a matter rest for the Burk must justify himself to the world and would eliminate any opposition in the process.

Their conversation had had as its background jolly cries of

revelry from below. Johnny's house garden was close to the foot of the Founder's Tower and there the house was gathering in festive mood. Johnny joined the party, distracted though he was by his thoughts, quietly though he would have preferred to slink off to his study and await the arrival of Jane. How could he possibly tell her of what the Burk called a 'malicious rumour' and which he, Johnny, was inclined to call the truth? He couldn't. But then it would be very difficult to suppress it in his own heart and mind – it would come between them and lurk below the surface until something would cause it to erupt, and then it would wreak havoc. That bastard bloody man!

As the party continued Johnny glanced up at the Founder's Tower, thinking of those two closeted together, Jane eagerly lapping up the phoney's words and encouragement. Don't listen to him, Jane. Don't listen to him! He's lying. He's your father and I can't bear it. What will you say, what will you think when you know? Come to me, get away from that grey contamination and put yourself in my arms!

She would come to him, he felt sure. She was more cautious now but there were still old boys around with girlfriends – some old members of the house with girlfriends were even joining in the celebration party here on the lawn so she would almost certainly make it undetected.

'Pray silence for the Headmaster,' bellowed the Horse as the Wolf climbed carefully up on a bench to express his personal congratulations to the house on their epoch-making victory of that afternoon.

'Boys,' he began in the hearty manner that normally forfeits the goodwill of its audience – though on this occasion the house was so pleased with itself it would have listened to anyone. 'This is very much a house occasion and I am privileged to be invited to share in your triumphal celebrations' (yeuch) 'but I can't pass over the opportunity to congratulate the house on this historic result. Not having won this particular trophy for... ' he turned to look down at the Horse standing respectfully on the lawn beside him – 'how long is it?... Yes, thank you, Mr Morse – fifty years! That means that anyone who had a grandfather in the house – is that anyone, by the way?' One or two hands went up reluctantly. 'Well, that means that you have redeemed your fathers in the eyes of your grandfathers! That's something to be proud of even in this modern age.' And on he went.

Eyes wandering – for what boy will voluntarily rest his gaze upon the visage of his headmaster for long? – Johnny found his attention wandering back to that high point in the Founder's Tower where he knew his beloved to be, and his heart yearned for her. But then his attention was attracted to a lower window in the building from which issued a thin trail of grey smoke. It was no more than might be caused by the burning of a piece of toast and Johnny watched it idly as a moderately interesting distraction from the Wolf's platitudes – 'the morale of every house depending crucially on... '

'Hey, look,' Johnny whispered, nudging his neighbour. For now the accident of burning the toast had unaccountably spread to another window, this time on the floor above. Furthermore, the window that first emitted the grey trail was now doing so with added thickness – in fact smoke was positively pouring upwards with a sort of hurried motion as if pursued. 'Christ, it's on fire!'

'Fire?' The buzz spread. The Wolf faltered, turned round to follow the direction of the common gaze. Even as he did so there was an exploding tinkle clearly audible to those below and a first floor window of the Tower gave dramatically outwards to release a sudden rush of dense grey smoke, this time accompanied at its centre by a momentary lick of flame.

'Phone for the Fire Brigade,' yelled the Wolf, quick to action in true headmasterly fashion. The Horse dashed inside to the housemasterly telephone.

Johnny was quicker. While to the other boys the burning down of the Founder's Tower would afford a spectacle of unparalleled excitement, to Johnny it was fraught with a terrible risk: his Jane was on the top floor. He raced away and through

the arch to the entrance to the Tower. He had no specific plan,
just a surge of purpose that shouted through his whole system
'Get to her – save her!' But any such hope was instantly dashed
by the sight that met his eyes as he approached the door.
Another master rushed by him coughing and Johnny saw that
the great wooden staircase up which he – and Jane – had so
recently made their way was richly ablaze: newel-post and
handrail, treads and risers were being fiercely gorged on by the
flames. Any nearer approach was unbearable and any ascent
impossible. And there was, Johnny thought, only one staircase
up the Tower, built as it had been long before the officious
interference of the fire authorities. Perhaps at second and third
– perhaps even fourth – floors there might be doors through to
adjoining buildings, but the fifth and sixth storeys were well
above the level of any others. A quick descent down a few
flights would provide escape for those on the top floor. But
what if the staircase was already filled with smoke by the time
they realised the danger and tried to head for safety? Johnny
imagined the Burk opening the door of his room to the inferno
outside and dashing back in to the desperate Jane. What could
they possibly do?

Johnny raced back to the house still gathered on the lawn.
Being separated from the great Tower only by a gravel drive,
the crowd had drawn back a bit now as the fire gained hold.
And the mood had changed. What had started as amused
excitement at the spectacle was changing to one of awe and
apprehension. As indeed it might, for although no pallid and
panicking faces had appeared at the windows – from which it
was generally assumed that either the Tower was empty of
occupants or that they had successfully escaped – the fire had
now got a tight and ferocious hold upon the building. From
most of the windows visible to the house party below flames as
well as smoke gushed, accompanied by a roaring noise that
struck terror into the assembled hearts, in none more than
Johnny's. That terror was immeasurably increased when with an
almost simultaneous gasp the crowd saw two figures suddenly

appear on the battlements.

'Christ, it's the Burk!'

'Who's that with him?'

Only Johnny knew.

'Where's the bloody fire engine? It's taking its time.'

Not only in Johnny's mind but probably in the Wolf's and the Horse's also was the terrible thought that the fire brigade, thinking they might be the victims of another hoax, were making their response with only moderate haste. But one look at the sky as they approached would quickly disabuse them of that idea.

At last the distant clanging of the longed-for bell was heard. The fire engine was approaching, but approaching with agonizing slowness. Through the arch it finally roared and swung to a standstill on the drive beside the house lawn. Its men, in helmets and waders for action, went about their business with practised and reassuring aplomb. The Wolf had rushed over to them on their arrival and was pointing upwards to the two figures on the battlements now only intermittently visible for the smoke that continued to billow into the clear evening sky. As a hose began to play upon the lower windows and a second engine appeared upon the scene the turntable ladder was brought laboriously into action, rising slowly into the sky and extending as it rose, a fireman perched courageously upon its tip. But alas! It was not long enough. This ladder was designed to achieve a height from which to pour down floods upon a three- or four-storey building and could not extend to the equivalent of five or six floors, the height from the ground at which Jane and the Burk now so perilously, and it seemed helplessly, stood.

And now a new and frightening feature lent added terror to their plight. 'Christ! The lead's melting!' As the smoke gushed upwards there began to trickle and then to pour downwards a river of grey – the lead with which the Tower was roofed and on which the now surely doomed figures perched. They had in fact climbed up to the highest point – the little circular platform on which the flagpole stood. To the flagpole they could be seen to cling, it was the last point of resort. But how long would it be before the heat had melted all the lead and the flames would burst through the wooden superstructure of the roof and engulf them both?

And then, just as they all realised that the best the fireman on the ladder could do was to play his hose upon the third and fourth floors, a new sound could be heard amongst the roar of the flames and of the fire engines – a deeper and louder roar of a mightier engine. A rhythmic whirring heralded the appearance immediately above their heads of a helicopter, a yellow coastguard helicopter that circled the scene slowly like some massive flying insect considering a flower, tilting and edging closer to the centre.

'It can't get near enough,' said a knowing voice in the crowd. Slowly, as it hovered above them, it let out a rope with, at its end, what must be some form of belt or harness. Unable for the heat and smoke to hover for more than a second or two above the blaze the helicopter had to make passes over it, the long rope being trailed over the heads of the two figures in their desperate plight. Several times the helicopter approached, the harness hanging, slowing as it passed over the Tower to make it that much more possible for them to grip the lifeline and so perhaps – if they could hold on – be saved. Several times the pleading hands rose pitifully in the air to grasp the elusive rope; several times the crowd rose in spirit as one to will the line of safety into their frantic reach.

At last, the lead flowing now in rivers down the side of the Tower and ominous crashings being heard from within, one frail female hand caught at the again-passing harness – and held. The helicopter, though shrouded in smoke, dipped to allow Jane to slip the belt about her waist before it tilted away, a body swinging now at last beneath it. With agonizing slowness but as safely as it could, the helicopter dropped gently over the house lawn, descending by degrees, till the rescued girl could be received into waiting hands and delivered from the saving harness. Jane was then safely in Johnny's arms.

Up went the harness again, to attempt its second life-saving mission. So preoccupied was Johnny with Jane – was she all right? could she breathe properly? was she burnt? – that he only belatedly became witness to the tragedy. What he did not see was the Burk getting his hand to the delivering harness and being, as Jane had been, pulled up to safety; what he did see was the terrible moment when, as the helicopter began to descend towards them, the Burk suddenly and inexplicably turned a somersault within the harness and slipped clean out of it, to plunge some fifty feet or so without restraint upon the unyielding surface of the house lawn. Despite her own ordeal, Jane was the first to him as he lay upon his back. She gently lifted the bald head and bent her ear to the slightly moving lips. Then, swiftly blanketed, the Burk was stretchered away to a waiting ambulance.

As the helicopter drew away and the fire engines began to get better control of the fire Jane, in Johnny's blazer, smudged and exhausted, clung to him and in her tears lifted her head to look at him and say, with a puzzled expression, 'He said 'Farewell, my child.' '

✻ EPILOGUE ✻
The Truth

Three weeks later there was a small gathering at the Rose and Crown at Bockington which consisted of Mrs Baxter and Jane, Johnny – and Mr Baxter, who was in a wheelchair, paralysed from the waist down and silent, but alive. Alive – unlike Derek Burkinshaw whose broken neck and back had had fatal consequences.

After a lot of post-fire stamping about by policemen and fire officers which the Headmaster would have liked to conceal from the boys but couldn't, he stated that the cause of the fire had not been determined absolutely but that it was thought to be an electrical fault. Such a momentous event could not in the boys' minds be satisfactorily accounted for in so mundane a way and there was plenty of gossip and speculation. Though one of the last to leave the Tower before the fire, Johnny was not under suspicion but he was in demand for his opinion and experience. Had he seen anything? Smelt anything? He couldn't say he had.

One of the most persistent rumours concerned Billy. At least one member of the school was willing to swear that he had seen that black figure coming up the back path some hours after he and Nick had been officially taxied away from the premises. Billy was famous for his unpredictable behaviour and even

Johnny couldn't entirely dismiss the idea of his friend committing arson. After all, he had earlier that day simply entered the Burk's room to retrieve his books and he had put on that inexplicable war dance on the occasion of the yobbo invasion. There was no telling what he might do.

However, as far as Johnny was concerned, there was a more important matter to clear up. Of Jane's parentage he was still – agonizingly – uncertain. He had felt that the terrible allegation was true and on top of that was the Burk's final words to Jane. Of course 'My child' was a term an adult could use of any young person and Johnny had passed it off as such on the bewildered Jane who was shocked enough already by the terror of the fire and her extraordinary escape. Her puzzlement at least showed that whatever the Burk had said to her on that fateful evening it did not touch on his relationship with her mother or his supposed relation to her. At least she'd been spared that horror. But in the circumstances the phrase suggested something more specific and Johnny feared the worst.

Round a table that had once, earlier that summer, been occupied by a platoon of thirsty and exhausted cadets sat Johnny and the Baxter family. The pub closed for the afternoon, they relaxed in the shade of the ash tree beside the stream. When Jane offered to wheel Mr Baxter down the lane Johnny took his courage in both hands and said, ' Mrs Baxter, about Mr Burkinshaw... erm, did you know him... before?'

Mrs Baxter smiled, knowing what the poor boy was after.

'Yes, of course you must be wondering. Well, when I was young,' she said, 'and working in a pub up north, where I come from, I met a young public school master who took a fancy to me. He seemed to be very clever and he wrote me poetry and I fell for him.' She smiled. 'You won't know another meaning – an old-fashioned meaning – of 'fell'. It means to become pregnant. Well, in those days, it was a shame and a disgrace to have a child out of wedlock; your reputation would never recover, you couldn't expect to make a decent marriage. You were done for – unless the man married you, 'made an honest woman of you', as the phrase went.'

'And you didn't marry?'

'No.'

'He wouldn't marry you?'

'And I wouldn't marry him. I was young – only seventeen. Lots of girls got married at around that age in those days but I knew it wouldn't be right for me. There only one respectable thing to do – in the unrespectable circumstances – and that was to go into a mother-and-baby home.'

'A mother-and-baby home?'

'Yes, a place where people in my situation went to have their babies before giving them up for adoption or taking them home and bringing them up alone.'

'Which did you do?'

'Neither. I couldn't face marriage and I couldn't face giving up my baby.'

'What about abortion?'

'Unthinkable in those days – at least amongst people of my family's type. If it was heard of it was done by mad hags in back streets with unsterilised instruments and was as likely to kill the mother as the baby.'

'What did your parents think you should do?'

'They wanted me to put it up for adoption; my Mum had some feeling for me, but my father was very angry.'

'So you... ?'

Mrs Baxter paused, with a heavy sigh. 'It's a long story.'

Which Johnny took to mean that she didn't really want to tell it, at least not then and there and certainly he had no right to press her.

'When Mr Baxter gave me the job here,' she however continued, 'and took me in, he soon saw what the problem was and we married. I fell in love with his kindness, I suppose. I didn't marry him for convenience. I loved him. I still love him and will to the day I die.'

'And then,' Johnny pursued tentatively, 'Jane was born.'

'And then,' said Mrs Baxter, 'the baby was born. But it was born dead – still-born. It never left the hospital.'

'So... ' Johnny began and stopped, letting this fact sink in.

'So my darling husband and I had another baby instead. And we called her Jane – after my grandmother.'

Johnny was silent. Mrs Baxter's grandmother seemed suddenly to him to be the grandest, loveliest old lady in the history of the world.

'You thought she really was Derek Burkinshaw's daughter, didn't you?' said Mrs Baxter, smiling again. 'So did Derek. No, that's not quite true. Of course he knew she couldn't be – the dates didn't fit. But he wanted to make up to me for it and wanted to do something to – what's the word? – get rid of the guilt he felt at what he had done to me. That's why he made such a fuss of her, as if she really were his daughter. I let him wriggle a bit – of course he must have known that I had a secret of his that wouldn't do his career any good if I let it out. Why shouldn't he suffer, I thought, after he had ruined me? He even offered to pay for some of her education at Worthington, and I was tempted. Of course, now he's dead I feel rather sorry about that and I'm glad that in the end I refused: I didn't want Jane indebted to him. And also he wasn't to know that he was actually driving me into the hands of a man far better than him. Poor Derek!' She smiled, looking at Johnny. 'You're a good boy, Johnny, and my Jane's a good girl. Stay good, won't you – for your own sake as well as for hers – not to mention mine!'

Johnny thought he knew what she meant and blushed crimson. 'And does Jane know about this?' he asked. 'About your... ?'

'Oh yes, she does now. Before, I thought there was no need for her to know, it would just be an embarrassment to her, and I suppose I was a bit ashamed of it too.'

'She was very confused when you met the B... Mr Burkinshaw at Worthington and suddenly went off the idea of her going there.'

'Yes, I know, but even then there was no need to give her the history. Anyway, I told her after the poor man died. I think she's forgiven me!'

They both watched Jane pushing her father back up the lane. She was smiling and chatting, though there could be no answering voice from him, and Johnny thought she was perfect and he couldn't possibly love her more than he did and would never ever do anything to harm her.

In mid-September the Michaelmas Term at Worthington started. Following the terrible accidental death of the Burk it was supposed that the 'girl operation' would be postponed. The Wolf, however, was not one to be deflected from his educational purpose by death or disaster and it was decreed that matters would go ahead all the same, though not quite as originally planned. The post of master-in-charge had to be reallotted and who more fitted for it than the Hawk, the benign and civilised Mr Hawke, with the pretty and astute wife? Nick's rooms were now required for refugees from the burnt-out Founder's Tower and so the girls – eventually few in number after all that had happened – began their Worthington careers in the distant safety of the Hawk's school house.

So under Mr and Mrs Hawke's careful eye Jane, rich in O Levels and endowed with a handsome scholarship (though untutored in Latin), lived in great contentment, throwing herself with relish into her studies and her sports, spending her time otherwise with her Johnny. His jealous fears had not been realised: the entire school had not, incomprehensible though it seemed to him, fallen in love with her, and indeed the two of them were swiftly recognised as 'a couple' and their relationship respected by all, not least the authorities who saw in them the early and gratifying flowering of the co-educational ideal. The Hawk and his wife took a special part-friendly, part-parental interest in the two of them under which they blossomed and flourished. The Horse reported favourably on a freshening in Johnny's academic effort – perhaps he would get to Oxford –

and on a maturing in his whole school outlook that would very likely put him in the running for the post of school prefect by half-term.

At last for Johnny and Jane then, their time was their own and they were free of fear and anxiety when they met. Holding hands in public – indeed any displays of affection – had been officially outlawed but the two found ample opportunity for as much contact as they wanted which commonly included kissing but had not yet gone on to the French variety or indeed to anything else. So a soft September afternoon might see them, hand in hand, cresting a spur of the Downs or crossing a golden stubble field under a kindly mackerel sky. From there they could gaze inland to the misted slopes beyond the Weald and eastwards to the grey of Bishopstown, fringing a blue sea. The world was all before them.

The first book in
THE SONS OF THE MORNING
sequence is
A STORM OF CHERRIES

In this story Johnny Clarke rises to the challenges of being Head
Boy at his prep school, The Dell. With a demanding headmaster, a
strong rival, a strange boy and an assistant master who does what
he shouldn't, his job is not an easy one; but, inspired by the
beautiful new matron, he sees it through to a triumphant
conclusion, though the fate of the school and of its headmaster is
not so rosy.

Popular Praise for
A STORM OF
❦ CHERRIES ❦

'…everything is as I remember it. You negotiate between the
ironic and affectionate with considerable skill, and… what really
impresses me is the way in which you manage to recreate the
child's eye view… I'm much looking forward to the further
adventures of Johnny Clarke.' JOHN MOLE

'It all brings back my preparatory school days. Happy as they were,
all the masters are living in your book.' PETER GORMLEY

'…very easy reading and compulsive to the end… you were
describing exactly my prep school and most of my experiences.'
JACK THOMAS

'Incredibly well-observed stuff: I loved it. I am very much looking
forward to the rest of the series.' NICHOLAS PATTERSON

'It is a fine piece of work: funny, deft, sad and spot-on true… you
have caught brilliantly the world of prep schools as they were.'
QUENTIN LETTS

'I was captivated by the story and the reminiscences it produced.'
MATTHEW FORSTER

Obtainable from WORDWISE, £7.99 including p&p
Brambles, Batts Lane, Pulborough RH20 2ED
Tel: 01798 875413 E-mail: wwordwise@aol.com
www.wordwisebooks.co.uk